SOLARIS FALL

A BEHEMOTH ASCENDING

NOVELLA

PART ONE

BY

FRANK J. MANCHON

*Con cariño de
tu amigo
Francisco Manchon*

Website: frankjmanchon.wordpress.com
Cover Design by Frank J. Manchon
Image used from Pixabay

This book is a work of fiction. Names, characters, places, and incidents are either products of the author's imagination or are used fictitiously. Any resemblance to actual events, locales, or persons, living or dead, is purely coincidental. All rights reserved. No part of this publication can be reproduced or transmitted in any form or by any means without permission in writing from the author.

Thanks to my family and friends, especially my wife, daughter and my parents-in-law for their support in this endeavour. I can't forget about two other people watching me from heaven: my dear sister and dad.

Table of Contents:

"We live in a society exquisitely dependent on science and technology, in which hardly anyone knows anything about science and technology."

Carl Sagan

SOLARIS FALL

BEHEMOTH ASCENDING NOVELLAS
PART ONE

PROLOGUE

High Commander Enki was in the Command Center of his flagship, the one-thousand-five-hundred-meter-long battleship *Thuban Executor*, waiting to exit hyperspace after weeks of endless travel. Enki was from a war-slaver reptilian-like race called *Thubans*, one of many that comprehended the *Draconian Empire*. Members of this race were, on average, eight to ten feet tall and did not have tails. Their skin was covered by thick, dark, green and black scales and they had dark yellow eyes. Like humans, they had five fingers. Their homeworld, *Thuban Prime*, was in a star cluster over eight hundred light years away.

Enki had, under his command, a powerful war fleet consisting of five battleships, eight battlecruisers, two battlecarriers and ten escort cruisers, all of them armed with beam cannons, laser turrets and deadly missiles with fifty-megaton war-heads.

His target was a triple star system, the Centaury System, where they had lost a slaved world of humanoids over four hundred years earlier, against a Starhuman fleet that had liberated the planet. After reconquering this world, Enki had one more mission, just four-and-a-half light years away: the golden planet, a world full of riches such as gold and other valuables.

"Status?" asked High Commander Enki in a deep voice, gazing at his Second Commander for a fast answer.

"Hyperspace drop out in two minutes," said Second Commander Marduk. "Scout ship reports no detection of Starhuman vessels in the system."

"Very well." Enki grinned. "Any other space activity that could endanger our fleet?"

"No, High Commander," Marduk said as he turned and looked at him. "The race that inhabits the only habitable world of the red dwarf star, the *Albeans*, a humanoid race with dark brown-red skin, has begun space exploration with rocket fuel vessels. I guess the

Starhumans helped them after we lost the system over four hundred years ago."

"They were a fine race for mining operations," responded Enki, thinking about how much it had costed him the loss of this galactic sector.

"They were indeed. In few more hours, they'll serve again our empire," added Marduk, showing his dark-blue poisonous tongue.

Four centuries earlier, a Starhuman fleet consisting of *Vegans* and *Lyrans* attacked and conquered a few of the Thubans slaved-worlds, such as the Albeans. The Vegan-Lyran fleet attacked many of the Thubans' slaved systems to paralyze their economy, freeing many of those worlds. It was a total success, as the Thuban economy almost went into bankruptcy. However, the worst loss was the golden planet, Terra, as the Starhumans named the blue-white globe, leaving the Thubans without their precious supplies of gold and slaves.

Thubans had a small empire that comprised more than fifty slaved-worlds of various humanoid and completely alien races, as well as a dozen worlds they inhabited. It took them almost four centuries to prepare and upgrade a fleet with the latest technology available in the empire.

-

In space, twenty-three Thuban ships exited hyperspace over two-hundred thousand kilometers away from the high-gravity planet of the Albeans in combat formation.

Enki felt a gut-stretching sensation when his battleship returned to normal space. It was a feeling he'd gotten used to, but it always bothersome.

"Take us over to the planet and nuke their primary cities," Enki ordered in a cold voice.

In the past, this world had given him a good slave race, and it was rich in minerals needed for ship construction. However, it wasn't rich in gold, as the precious yellow metal was found very deep beneath the planet's crust, which made mining impractical.

"On our way, High Commander," replied Second Commander Marduk. "Are you not concerned about the losses we may have if we nuke the planet? High levels of radiation are lethal for our kind."

"I am very aware of that," said Enki dismissively. He knew that he could bring slaves from other worlds and even replace this race with another. "This is a lesson they must learn. They must know that if anything happens to us, they are to pay for it."

"I am sure you are right, High Commander," responded Marduk, letting out a deep and resigned breath.

It was the job of the Second Commander to point out suggestions that might persuade the High Commander that he was making the wrong decisions.

Enki touched his claws one to the other. "I grow impatient to taste the blood of the humans we genetically created two hundred thousand years ago. It has been so long since their blood ran out in the *butcher houses.*"

Marduk nodded.

"One can find it in the black markets of the Sozarians pirates' worlds," Marduk suggested. "I heard it's costly to acquire a pill of human hormones but prohibitively expensive to buy a small tubule of blood. They could cost over a hundred thousand *draks.*"

In the known universe, gold and other valuables were used as currency. The name of the money varied depending on the sector of the galaxy or universe in which it was used. Some called it *credits*, others called it *scripts*, but Draconians had named it *draks*.

Enki's eyes grew wide in anger. He hated that his crew frequented those worlds to spend their share of gold or *draks*, so hardly earned. "And how do you know that?"

Marduk held his breath, unsure of what to say. "A friend of mine who works in another fleet used to go there," he replied, his gaze lost in the data on his tactical display.

"You'd better watch your back. If I find out you went there without my permission, you are as good as dead," Enki threatened with a dark look in his reptilian eyes. "Anyway, how do the pirates have stock of those products?"

"Unknown, High Commander. If I were to guess, they may have raided the golden planet, abducting a few dozens of humans at the time and slowly draining their blood, making sure they don't die right away."

"We may have to do the same," responded Enki.

-

President K'sel of the Albeans was in shock when his Secretary of Defense, General Kenne, informed him of an alien fleet approaching the planet. For the last four hundred years, the Albeans had lived in peace but in a constant state of alert. They knew the Thubans would return eventually, though they held out a small hope that this day would never arrive.

"How many ships?" President K'sel asked, his expression deeply concerned.

"At least twenty, Mr. President," replied General Kenne. "Our telescopes detected an anomaly in space, and our scientist cataloged it as hyperspace vortexes. We do know the ancient enemy possessed such technology."

K'sel remained silent for a moment. "Why did our ancestors refuse the Starhuman Alliance aid?"

"I guess, Mr. President, that our ancestors didn't want to change one oppressor for another," answered Kenne, citing what the military academy had taught him when he was just a cadet. "We didn't know the Starhumans enough to accept their offer of military assistance."

"I understand your views, but now we're alone and defenseless," K'sel said, his gaze alight with fear. "Perhaps we wouldn't be in this situation if they had accepted their offer. Our technology would be much more advanced than it is now."

"With your approval, we can launch our ground nuclear missiles. A preventive attack against the enemy could give us a deterrent effect. Perhaps they will withdraw," Kenne said firmly. It was his duty, as the Secretary of Defence, to do whatever was possible to safeguard his race. "We need to act now, or the enemy will be here soon."

President K'sel thought about the consequences of such an action. He knew that doing nothing was as bad as doing it. Then he decided. "Here, you have my authorization codes. Launch the missiles."

"Yes, Mr. President," Kenne said when he took out a black briefcase. Once it was open, a small panel display was visible. The General inserted the two code cards into the slots and activated them. "Your move, Mr. President."

"The Gods protect us," K'sel said, pressing the red button.

-

One hour later, High Commander Enki gazed at the helpless planet in his viewscreen. It was a beautiful world, something the Thubans didn't care about. They were a race of scavengers, preying on lesser civilizations for a quick reward in the form of slaves, gold and minerals.

The fleet rapidly approached the planet. High Commander Enki ignored radio transmissions with frantic pleas for peace.

"Attack the planet. I grow impatient to depart to our primary target, the golden planet," Enki said, his eyes showing greed.

"*Raptor* fighters and *Tyrannous* bombers launched," said Second Officer Ynnie, his eyes focused on the tactical viewscreen showing green icons advancing toward the planet.

"High Commander," said Sensor Officer Okyd in confusion. "I detect more than a hundred red icons exiting the planet's atmosphere!"

"What are they?" Enki asked, completely perplexed. Perhaps this mission wouldn't be as easy as he'd previously thought.

Okyd seemed to calm down as the sensor scan showed the data readings of the inbound objects. "Nuclear missiles powered by fossil fuels. No harm in them."

"Very well," Enki answered in relief. "Order the fighters to shoot them down."

-

In space, *Raptor* fighters were closing the distance with the Albeans missiles. It was a terrible mistake on the part of this race to attack the Thuban fleet, as this transgression wouldn't remain unpunished.

Missile after missile was shot down by the reptilian semi-circular fighters in clamps maneuvers, making short work of it.

After a few minutes, bright explosions were visible in low orbit of the planet as one hundred and five nuclear missiles were destroyed. Nothing remained of the rockets, just debris that would enter the planet's atmosphere in the next few hours.

-

In the administrative building of the Albean capital, President K'sel remained silent as every nuclear missile was shot down. In the situation room, everyone's nerves were on edge.

More than three billion Albeans inhabited the planet, and once again, they were about to be conquered by the Thubans. K'sel remembered very well what the aliens had done in the past, but his people refused to be occupied by Starhuman forces to safeguard their planet. It was a bad decision on the part of his ancestors, one that would undoubtedly result in another brutal alien occupation. The only help they had accepted from the Starhumans was technology. Over the course of four hundred years, the Albeans had passed from an iron-age agricultural society to rocket fuel space exploration. They had more technology available to them, but it was too late; the Thubans were back, and they would need another hundred years to implement such advanced technology.

"Mr. President, we have received a video message from the Thuban High Commander," said Secretary of Defense General Kenne.

"Play it on the main screen," ordered President K'sel, his face turning pale.

On the main screen, a reptilian face appeared. It was High Commander Enki. "Fool Albeans, because of your missile attack, half of your major cities will be nuked. This world is no longer yours; it's mine now. Remember that before you do something else stupid."

Everyone remained silent, a cold chill running through their bodies.

"What are we to do, Mr. President?" asked General Kenne, his expression deeply concerned. "More than three hundred million people live in those cities."

"We are doomed," replied the president, his gaze showing defeat. Then a bright light illuminated the room and everyone inside was incinerated as a fifty-megaton nuclear warhead detonated over the capital city.

-

High Commander Enki was pleased with the attack. He knew that he had lost millions of potential slaves, but he had set an example for the future. If this race rebelled rebel against their new masters, the punishment would be severe.

"Begin the invasion. Annihilate any resistance. In two days, an occupation force will arrive. Then we'll depart to the golden planet," said Enki with a grin on his reptilian face.

First Officer Ebagesh, leader of the invasion troops, nodded. "It will be done, High Commander."

CHAPTER ONE

There was always a romantic vision of the universe and traveling to the stars. Through a human eye, the stars were the beyond, the place where the Gods lived. In a certain way, they did live there.

Many alien races populated the known galaxy, the Milky Way. Some of those races were humanoid, resembling normal Earth humans. However, they did not originate in this galaxy but, rather, somewhere else. No one knew how or why humans had appeared in this galaxy. Most of the advanced human-like races didn't believe in a God, but in an ancient race with powers resembling those of a God – a race that created all life in this galaxy and possibly in others. That ancient mythical race had seeded numerous planets across the galaxy with humanoid life-forms. The reason why this race had done so was unknown but the proof that it had, in fact, done so was certain, as geneticists had found a common ancestor in the DNA of every humanoid race discovered in the known galaxy.

A few humanoid species formed the *Starhuman Alliance*, a type of trade federation composed of the arrogant *Lyrans*, the complacent *Vegans*, the pacifist *Syrians*, and the enlightened *Pleiadeans*. They sought the advancement and enlightenment of all human races across the galaxy. Starhumans wasn't an armed society, but they possessed a powerful fleet built by necessity, as enemies were increasing in every corner of the universe. Lyrans had the biggest fleet in the Alliance, numbering in the thousands, and Vegans in lesser numbers to protect their trade routes from pirates.

The Pleiadeans had one of the most advanced and powerful fleets in the galaxy, though it wasn't as big as that of the Lyrans. They used it only as a deterrent against any threat to their worlds.

The Starhuman Alliance changed its peaceful path when the Draconian Empire attacked it.

Hundreds of thousands of years earlier, the Starhuman Alliance and the reptilian Draconian Empire had begun a cruel war after a misunderstanding during a first-contact scenario. The Draconians found a Lyran colony in their ravenous search for new worlds with which to feed their enormous and rapidly growing population. The Lyrans didn't trust them and wanted to know more before reaching an agreement. The Draconians took that answer as an offense and initiated an attack against a peaceful and agricultural Lyran colony, destroying it and killing more than two hundred million inhabitants. Since then, both races had been at war.

The Draconian Empire was another loose federation of diverse reptilian races divided into clans and castes. The Draconians were a militaristic empire with one goal: seek, destroy and enslave humanoid races. The significant groups were the *Ciakans*, the *Saurians*, the *Dracons* (from which the Empire took its name) and the *Gorgons*. Empress Ishtar, an almost immortal queen, had ruled the empire with an iron hand for millennia.

There were other minor clans, such as the Thubans. Their homeworld was Thuban Prime, located in a star cluster over eight hundred light years away toward the galactic center.

The Thubans were scavengers and preyed on lesser civilizations for their resources and the most critical thing for them: slaves for manual labor and humanoid blood to be sold in the *butcher houses*. Thuban Prime was far from the empire, almost a thousand light years from the capital world, Ciakar.

-

Consul Atlas sat in a wooden chair, enjoying the spring morning in his garden. In the blue sky, a comet with a long tail was visible. It was a regular visitor that passed by Terra every few hundred years. Atlas gazed at the comet and took a sip of his tea. He continued watching the birds and small insects filling the numerous exotic plants, flowers and small trees, including the many varieties of fruit trees and palms that covered the vast palace garden. He loved palms; the coconut variety was his favorite, as it reminded him of the trees back on Helix. Every day for the last few centuries, he had remembered his childhood in his homeworld, Atlantea. It was a beautiful world, eighty percent of which was covered with deep blue oceans. One land mass sat in the equatorial area of the planet, as did scattered islands. Sadly, the Earth-like world had been incinerated by the Helix star that, without warning, had entered during a nova phase.

Atlas was enjoying his cup of hot tea, lost in his memories. when Commodore Valentis suddenly appeared in an apparent hurry.

"Commodore, what a beautiful day," Atlas said, sipping his tea. "What's the rush?"

"Consul." Valentis militarily saluted him, letting out a deep and ragged breath. "Orbital satellites just picked this up from the edge of the Solaris System." He gave Atlas a small device showing the anomaly in space.

"According to our specialists, these could be hyperspace exiting vortexes."

Atlas remained quiet for a moment, taking another sip of his drink. "Perhaps the fleet we sent to aid the Syrians against the pirates is back."

"No, Consul. If that were the case, we could pick up their transponder signatures." Valentis took a deep breath before continuing. "I think they're back, and that anomaly is the beginning of an invasion fleet."

"Do not get too far ahead of yourself, Commodore. I am sure there is a rational explanation for that event, and that it is nothing to worry about. Please sit and have a cup of tea with me. This variety is delicious!"

"With all due respect, Consul, we should activate the military immediately, before it's too late," Valentis said, showing disbelief at the way the Consul was acting.

Atlas straightened himself in his chair and looked straight into Valentis' eyes. "My dear friend, how long have we known each other?

Valentis remained silent for a few seconds, trying to determine where the Consul was going with that question in a moment of maximum alert. "Over one hundred Terran years, sir,"

"Exactly," Atlas replied, holding his cup. "In all this time, how many times have I been wrong?"

Valentis began feeling uncomfortable in the surreal situation. "Sir, I do not know where you are going with this, but we must declare a state of emergency, even if it's only a precaution. We must be ready. If these are hyperspace vortexes, an enemy fleet could be here in a matter of hours. Do you understand me, Consul?

Atlas nodded. "Perhaps you are right, Commodore. Do as you consider necessary."

At times, Commodore Valentis thought that the Consul was senile and that an early retirement from political activities was necessary.

-

For the last four hundred years, the city of Atlantis had flourished in peace on the north-west coast of the Libyan continent, built in a series of concentric rings in a shallow sea that engulfed the continental area. It was surrounded by tall mountains and green and fertile plains that were full of life. It was also rich in natural resources. Atlanteans weren't from Terra, as they named the planet; they were from a distant world over six hundred light years away, in the Helix System.

This human race were descendants of the Vegans, but a supernova had destroyed their world. They found Terra occupied by the Thubans. What the Atlanteans found out after driving them away from Terra was that they had enslaved the native human population, forcing them to extract gold and other valuables from the mines. The natives also said the reptilians used to sacrifice them and drink the blood of the victims to renew their power. Such stories horrified the current Atlantean leader, Consul Atleanis, grandfather of Consul Atlas. Most shocking to him were the child sacrifices that the evil aliens practiced.

After years of investigation, the Atlanteans discovered that the natives weren't a casual evolutionary product of nature; they had been genetically created by the reptilians to serve them as slaves. In the natives' DNA, they found traces of Lyran, Vegan and Syrian genetic codes mixed to create a superhuman species capable of hard work in adverse and harsh conditions.

One thing shocked the Atlanteans scientists: A small proportion of DNA, less than one percent, was reptilian. That discovery meant the new human race, named by the reptilians as *Adamu*, was very aggressive and warlike. When the Atlanteans found Terra, the world was in a state of insurrection. Some native civilizations revolted against their creators and masters, all of them fighting with iron weapons and stolen alien rifles.

Atlanteans had another city in the middle of the ocean, Poseidonia, two thousand kilometers away, located in a beautiful archipelago where the military and the scientific installations were located. Atlanteans didn't want too much involvement in Terra, as the planet belonged to the natives, but they wanted a gradual advancement of the civilizations on the earth to interbreed with them and, one day, form a new civilization with Atlantean culture and technology.

-

High Commander Enki was in the Command Center of his flagship, the one-thousand-five-hundred-meter-long battleship *Thuban Executor*, waiting to exit hyperspace in the Solaris System. Terra's natives knew them as *Anunnaki*, but different terms were also in use, such as *Nephilim*, *The Fallen* or *Evil Ones*.

The Thubans were a shape-shifting race thanks to their advanced genetic technology, which they used to trick some of the humanoid worlds, pretending to be their gods. At Terra, they adopted the appearance of humans with beards, making it more natural for the natives to accept their dominance.

Two hundred thousand years earlier, they had arrived at Terra, founding a primitive race of hominids that resembled the empire's ancient enemy, the Starhumans, though in an early stage of evolution. Thubans attempted to enslave the cavemen, but they couldn't work the mines, as their primitive brains didn't understand the orders they received. After several years spent training the primates and failing miserably in the endeavor of extracting the gold that the Thubans needed, the Thuban Council agreed to modify them so that they qualified to work in the mines; thus, *Homo sapiens* was born.

Discrepancies arose in the Council, as the idea of giving advanced intelligence to those inferior apes could be worrisome in the future if it was handled hastily. Another reason for the genetic engineering was the following: Thubans fed themselves with humanoid flesh and blood, changing the course of the world forever.

"We just exited hyperspace, High Commander, outside the gravity well of the eighth planet," reported Second Officer Ynnie after they had dropped out of hyperspace in a far sector of the system, as a precaution.

"Excellent," said Commander Enki in a deep and sharp voice after the stretching-gut sensation had vanished. "Set course to the third planet of this system. Let's see if there are Starhumans there interfering with our gold and slave supplies, as Exploration Commander Ulbaral has reported. I reckon that what he discovered was just a patrol fleet."

One scout ship had scanned Solaris System a few years earlier, with disturbing results: Starhumans were in the system. Exploration Commander Ulbaral waited out of the system, in the Kuiper Belt, when the scout returned with the bad news. Acting immediately, Ulbaral departed to Thuban Prime, where High Commander Enki was finalizing the preparations for his new and updated fleet.

"Course set," Ynnie replied, pressing icons in his tactical display.

"Sensors indicate numerous civilian spacecraft in the third and fourth planets, possibly of Vegan design, and four warships, heavy destroyer class," said Sensor Officer Okyd.

"Damn Vegans!" grumbled Enki, infuriated. "Set fleet in battle condition. Let's destroy those damn bastards!"

"Fleet in battle condition, Commander!" Ynnie reported.

"They're more advanced than we are," said Second Commander Marduk, concern in his voice. "They could easily drive us out of this system forever. Remember, they have hundreds of systems, including the Pleiadeans as allies. No one wants to engage in battle with a Pleiadean vessel, not even a Lyran one!"

"They're far out of their region of space and our latest reports showed that the Starhumans are more divided than previously thought. Our intelligence services, with the help of the Sozarians pirates, believe that each of their worlds is independent and that the only tie with the alliance is purely for trade. They've joined their military forces together on only a few occasions, with an exception being our defeat four hundred years ago. We need the gold of this planet and the slave race we genetically modified to work in the mines," Enki replied, frowning in anger. "Without that gold, our planet's atmosphere will disappear in a few years, and our people will die."

Thuban Prime had experienced an atmospheric problem for centuries. They had polluted so much of the planet, gold was needed to keep the solar radiation from sterilizing the planet's surface and converting the Thubans' homeworld, once a blue-white globe, into a barren wasteland.

"We could always resettle another planet or steal the atmospheric retention fields from these Vegans. We know from the same pirates that Vegans possess such technology. Just think about how much gold we could have if we didn't have to vaporize it in our homeworld atmosphere," Marduk answered, worrying about the consequences of such a suggestion.

"Watch your words, Second Commander. You are talking about our homeworld, and that is sacred!" Enki said, gazing straight into Marduk's reptilian eyes.

In just a few hours, High Commander Enki could finally get the victory he needed from his eternal enemies, who would pay a high price for interfering in his claimed sector of the galaxy. He would get control of the gold planet.

CHAPTER TWO

I n the fourth planet of Solaris, as the Atlanteans had baptized this star system, a colony of more than one million people flourished.

Mars was a barren world, but it hadn't always been like that. Hundreds of millions of years earlier, the planet had plenty of water, a thick atmosphere and life. However, everything changed when a planetoid the size of Terra's moon collided with it, altering the molten core and mantle of the planet. Slowly it solidified and Mars lost its magnetic field, leaving the atmosphere without a possible defense against the cosmic radiation which stripped most of it away from the planet into the vacuum of space.

Deep beneath the surface, in Mariner Valley, Atlanteans built a large piece of machinery, so technologically advanced that it could bring the planet back to life, making Mars a garden once again. The device was called the *Titan Project*, and it was a huge laser cannon powered by antimatter that shot into the solid outer core and melted it. Firing enough energy in a determined frequency into the solid external base, this one, in a matter of time, would dissolve and become liquid again, initiating, like that, the rotation between the outer and the inner core. Atlanteans had never done this, but Lyrans did it with fabulous results. Mars was perfect for it, except for its low gravity – only a third of Terra's normal one. Terraforming technology in the Starhuman Alliance was among the most advanced in the known galaxy, and the new developments in gravitational fields were instrumental to the ability of planets, like Mars, to avoid health problems among a population that had grown up in a low-gravity world. Most worlds in the alliance were almost like Terra in size and gravity. They had plans for terraforming Venus in the future, but they needed further technological developments.

"Status of the Titan Cannon?" Commander Padis asked, his gaze checking the data from the last test.

Padis was a veteran of the last war and now acted as Governor of Mars. He was over five hundred years old, but he looked like an earthling in its forties. That was the result of thousands of years of genetic manipulation. Vegans could live a long and healthy life for over eight hundred years. They knew no illness. Only one thing could end their lives before their natural life span: the war with the Draconian Thubans.

"Ready for a new test at your order, Commander," Vera replied in a soft voice.

Vera was the AI in charge of the Titan Project. She seemed as human as Padis was. If one day she decided to get a body, she could transfer her program to a synthetic one, but so far, she had refused. The procedure was called *Soul Transferring* and the plastic bodies they used were utterly bionic. All Starhuman allies used AIs to maximize the productivity and efficiency of the systems. None of the worlds in the alliance did any manual labor for millennia, leaving AIs and work robots in charge of everything. It was a system that worked for them, but it had its problems: Humans became complacent and weak. Vera had a holographic 3D display all over the complex. She could materialize herself anywhere, and she looked as real as a human. Vera resembled a young woman in her twenties, with long, dark hair and deep black eyes. Her skin was tan-brown. She wore a white uniform with red lines along the sides of the trousers. That was the standard uniform for officers in the Vegans' fleet. Only forty crew members operated the largest ships of the fleet: the dreadnoughts battleships.

"Set up a new test in the next thirty minutes, this time at full power," Padis ordered.

He wanted to see the full potential of the cannon. If this last test were successful, Mars' outer and inner core would be fully functional again in months. The population would be safe in the dome cities, protected by a powerful energy screen. No marsquake or volcanic eruption, such as Arsia or Olympus Mons lava, could penetrate it.

"Final test ready in thirty minutes," answered Vera in her melodic voice.

In the last test, the cannon melted an area of one hundred kilometers around the valley. The idea was to heat that molten metal into a state of near plasma, thereby triggering a chain reaction that would affect the whole planet. Nevertheless, this mechanism had some side effects: Marsquakes and volcanic activity could engulf the world during years of instability, but it was necessary to build a thick atmosphere and a magnetic field. Nonetheless, something else was missing for creating a garden: water.

"Commander!" shouted Larissa, the communication operator, her eyes alight with fear. "We have reports of a Draconian fleet between Neptune and Uranus. They exited hyperspace over ten minutes ago."

"Damn! Abort test and evacuate the civil population to the underground bunkers of the complex. Order the military to be deployed and launch fighters," Padis ordered, his face showing a frightened look.

They didn't expect the Draconian to show up at that moment. He wondered from where this fleet had come. If the reports were accurate, the Draconians were retreating for the last centuries of war. It seemed the latest news about the Draconian-Starhuman Alliance war was wrong.

-

Back in Atlantis, at the center of the ringed island formation, Consul Atlas was in the situation room of the Command Center and Government Palace, which the governmental powers inhabited.

"Situation report, Commodore?" asked Consul Atlas of Commodore Valentis, the Commander in Chief of the Atlanteans' military forces.

"Twenty-three enemy vessels have been detected between Neptune and Uranus and are advancing rapidly. Estimated engagement time is twelve hours," Valentis reported, staring at the Consul. He had warned him of this outcome, but the old man hadn't wanted to listen. Now they were in a precarious situation. Over the last century, Valentis has requested the construction of new warships and shuttles to evacuate the whole population if needed. However, every time, his requests had been refused by the Consul and his cronies, all of whom were in an age of complacent and accustomed to luxury. He knew well that his race didn't have a chance in a long-term war against any adversary, as they had grown weak over thousands of years.

Atlas nodded, his eyes lost in the shrews. "Who are they?"

"Mars is informing that the enemy is a Draconian fleet, possibly Thubans," Valentis stated with a deep sigh. "Their long-range sensors are much better than ours are."

The Consul turned his gaze toward Senator Tyron. "We need more information."

Senator Tyron was Atlas' civilian personal adviser – another crooked politician, according to Valentis' standards. "I suggest sending a diplomatic mission to the Thubans; I feel they're more reasonable than we have believed before."

Valentis couldn't believe what he was witnessing. "Are you losing your mind? Don't you know who the Draconians are?"

"These are the Thubans!" uttered Senator Tyron with a closed fist. "We must try every diplomatic channel possible before we send our fleet!"

"What fleet?" Valentis retorted. "We have four destroyers with personnel ever proven in battle, not to mention the fact that our more powerful vessels are light years away, aiding the Syrians against some pirates' gunships. How many times did I request warship construction? Why the hell did we build a space station over Mars? I guess you all know the answer: for nothing."

"Enough!" Atlas shouted, gazing at both furious men. "Any vessels in the area?"

Valentis shook his head in disbelief. "No, sir, the nearest ones are tug-crafts in the rings of Saturn, bringing water-ice to Mars."

More than five hundred small tug-crafts were deployed between the asteroid belt and the rings of Saturn to bring small asteroids with a significant amount of water-ice or just pure chunks of it, launching them in a shallow trajectory against the planet's atmosphere to melt the water.

With narrowed eyes, Sensor Officer Allumin turned his face toward Commodore Valentis. "We have a freighter approaching Ceres, the *Agincourt*. It could intercept the enemy fleet near Jupiter in four hours if we send it now."

Valentis remained silent for a moment, considering the proposal. He knew the only way to impeach the

Consul was with the support of over sixty percent of the cabinet. However, the Consul had bought every single member with bribes and opulent luxuries. He stepped over to the officer's display and studied the data. "Do it," he ordered, now gazing Consul Atlas. "Sir, I recommend ordering a complete telecommunication blackout in every mining operation and scientific post across Solaris. Perhaps the enemy won't attack them."

Atlas nodded in agreement. "It's prudent and wise that we do so. Nara, send the orders."

Comm Officer Nara nodded, then pressed some icons on her tactical display. "Orders sent, Consul," she said softly.

-

On board the *Thuban Executor*, High Commander Enki watched the tactical display that monitored all Starhuman vessels. There weren't many of them; most were just cargoes or freighters transporting raw materials and water-ice from the outer planet's rings.

"Damn Vegans! They think this solar system is theirs!" Enki shouted, spitting on the metal ground.

"High Commander, I think they're terraforming the fourth planet. Those small tug-crafts are transporting big pieces of water-ice and launching them into the planet's atmosphere. I also detect some movement in the outer and inner cores of the planet," reported Second Commander Marduk as he read his tactical viewscreen.

Enki remained thoughtful for a few moments, then replied, "Send the *Ascendant Ripper* and the *Behemoth Ascending* with a few escort cruisers. Once we pass the fifth planet's orbit, annihilate every human in that world. We must not let them have a second blue-white world here."

"High Commander, with all due respect, we could use that planet for ourselves as a military base," Marduk said, fearful of the High Commander.

Marduk had a problem, and that was honesty, which was very rare among Thubans.

Wrath filled High Commander Enki's gaze. "We don't need a planet like that one, small and with low gravity. We don't need a planet at all. We need their inhabitants as a food source, slave labor and their gold! That's all. However, for this, we must annihilate the goddamn Vegans. They can no longer serve as slaves; they must die."

Marduk remained silent for a long moment. He had to learn how to shut his mouth. With a regretful look, he turned to his tactical display and sent the orders to the two-thousand-meter-long battle carrier *Ascendant Ripper* and the one-thousand-and-two-hundred-meter-long heavy battlecruiser *Behemoth Ascending*. "Orders sent, High Commander. Escort cruisers *Bastion*, *Khoda* and *Qwarda* will join the two ships. Six hours for departure at current speed."

"Very well," Enki said with satisfaction. He would finally get his revenge against these humans.

Enki had been at the last battle over four hundred years ago, when he saw his fleet annihilated in a matter of seconds. At that moment, the Thubans' war fleets didn't possess an energy screen. Other Draconian fleets did have shields and mighty ones, but Thubans only preyed on lesser civilizations with no technological development. That was the case with the Terrans, semi-sentient creatures who served as food and slaves.

At the last moment, Enki had escaped in a cargo ship full of gold. That gold, and the previously extracted goal, was valued in the trillions of *draks*. It helped him to upgrade his new fleets with better weapons and technology. Thubans were very aggressive. It was their way, but they could also be very patient if revenge was involved – and this was the case. The Starhumans were about to pay for their excessive meddling.

"High Commander, I detect a vessel is coming toward us," Sensor Officer Okyd reported.

"What type?" Enki asked.

Okyd gazed at the High Commander in disbelief. "It's a freighter."

"Is it armed?" asked Enki, his eyes showing confusion.

"Unarmed," Okyd responded.

"Why would they send an unarmed vessel toward us? That's suicide!" Marduk muttered.

"We'll find out soon enough," replied Enki, his eyes focusing on the inbound vessel.

CHAPTER THREE

One million kilometers from Jupiter, the Atlantean freighter *Agincourt* was approaching the Thuban battlefleet.

"Status?" asked Captain Nardoll, sitting in his chair at the freighter's Command Deck.

"Approaching the enemy fleet at ten percent sublight. Estimate contact time in fifteen minutes. Without visual, we won't be able to send a message, as the enemy is behind the planet. Sensors scan determined they will be out of the curvature of the gas giant in a few more minutes," stated XO Deinn, touching several icons on his viewscreen.

Nardoll nodded. "Place the ship near Europa. If we get attacked, perhaps the moon will serve as protection."

"Sir, we don't have an FTL drive. If something goes wrong, we're as good as dead," Deinn said, his eyes showing concern.

"Those damn politicians, always sending others to do their goddamn job!" moaned Navigation operator

Gosar, chewing a bit of tobacco. That was one thing Terra possessed: a high-quality tobacco plant, cannabis.

"We serve to our worlds, Gosar. Don't start with one of your political rallies about workers' rights and paychecks," said Captain Nardoll. He knew that Gosar was right but he was the Captain and he had to maintain order on his ship.

The *Agincourt* was an old ice-hauler that captured ice from the rings of Saturn and delivered it to Mars for human consumption. Mars had water beneath its surface, but it was primarily salted and difficult to extract. Hauling water was much more comfortable and economical.

Gosar continued his claims against Atlantean politics and laws. "Our race lost its vitality. Bloody machines and AIs do all the work, leaving our people complacent and bored with arts and science. Even having a child isn't natural anymore!"

Captain Nardoll nodded in agreement. It was better to agree with a fool than to argue with one. "You are right; when we get back to Mars, you can write another letter to Governor Padis about your claims."

"To the Governor?" Gosar asked with a laugh. "I will present myself in the Government Palace in Atlantis! I will shake that place until they open their shit-covered eyes! Did you see what kind of places they live in? Huge palaces with all kind of foods and luxuries while we're here eating dry food and sleeping with giant space rats! Those damn rodents are enormous because of the lack of gravity! We don't even have a gravity generator! My bones are getting as damn thin as pap!"

"The only thing that will shake it will be your body after you're stunned by a combat robot, you idiot!" XO Deinn said, gazing at the political agitator. "Go back to work. We're approaching short communication range. Otherwise, you'll get a monthly deduction in your wages!"

Gosar nodded. "Aye, XO, as you command! However, remember that one day the machines will take us over! They don't need us because we're just a bunch of lazy sacks of bones and meat!"

One thing was for sure: Gosar loved money more than anything else. It was one way to shut his mouth, treating him with a wage deduction.

-

Minutes passed and the *Agincourt* was in communication range with the Thuban fleet. Tension grew across the Command Deck of the old ice-hauler.

"Do you think they're going to shoot us down?" XO Deinn asked the Captain.

Nardoll was intently reading the message he had to broadcast to the reptilian fleet. It was a truce treaty. For Nardoll, that meant one thing: the government didn't believe they could win. "Let's think positively," he whispered, unsure of what to say. Then he pressed the comm button of his panel. "Here we go. Captain Nardoll of the ice-hauler freighter *Agincourt* to the Commander in Chief of the Draconian Fleet. This message is on behalf of the Atlantean Government. Do not shoot us down. We're an unarmed civilian vessel on a diplomatic mission. The Atlantean Government proposes a truce, a ceasing of hostilities between our races. We can reach an agreement if we follow the path of peace," Nardoll read in an assuring voice, though he didn't believe a word of it.

Gosar gazed at the Captain in total disbelief. "A fucking truce? Are they bloody serious? Where is the damn fleet? Alternatively, the Lyrans? Those damn arrogant idiots can't see beyond their belly buttons!"

"Shut up, man!" growled XO Deinn. "Shut the fuck up!

-

High Commander Enki was laughing out loud in his Command Chair. Starhumans always tried to negotiate if they were on the losing end. That message made the High Commander confident in his victory. "Fool

Vegans!" Enki said with a grin. "Destroy that vessel. That will be our answer to their foolish pleas."

"As you wish, High Commander," Marduk replied, pressing the missile launching button on his tactical display. "Missiles launched. Three minutes to impact if they don't use that moon to hide."

-

In the Command Deck of the ice-hauler *Agincourt*, Captain Nardoll was in shock and fright. Four missiles left the tubes of what looked to be the flagship of the enemy fleet. "Move us out of here! Take the ship behind the moon!" shouted Nardoll, his frightened face turned pale.

"Course set. Hold tight. This will be a high G maneuver!" XO Deinn said in a frantic voice. He manually took the controls of the ship. The *Agincourt* began descending, seeking protection behind the icy moon.

"I curse our damn government!" Gosar said, checking his navigation screen to see that the four missiles were on different trajectories, surrounding the moon. "We're dead!"

"Come on, you damn old piece of wreckage!" Deinn shouted, his chest feeling tremendous pressure of over eight G's as he moved the controls of the ship to descend toward the moon.

-

In space, around the moon Europa, four Thuban missiles were approaching the Atlantean vessel *Agincourt*. Each rocket took a different path to ensure the ice-hauler didn't escape. The freighter, making evasive maneuvers, was descending toward the south pole of the moon, gaining speed in a slingshot procedure. Suddenly, all missiles failed in their mission to destroy the Atlantean vessel. They flew by the moon and exploded because they'd lost their target.

"Yeah!" XO Deinn screamed in jubilation. "We lost them!

"Get us out of here, full sub-light speed," Captain Nardoll ordered with relief, though he still worried about how they would escape.

When the missile-locked alarm stopped sounding in the Command Deck of the *Agincourt*, another danger appeared. Just in front of the ice-hauler, a one-thousand-and-two-hundred-meter-long battlecruiser stood still over the south pole of the moon, waiting for the Atlantean vessel to show up; it was the *Behemoth Ascending*.

"Where the fuck did that thing came from?" Gosar asked, his breath quickening.

"Evasive maneuvers, now!" Captain Nardoll ordered.

It was too late.

Bright blue and white beams fired from the Thuban battlecruiser to tear apart the Starhuman freighter. In a second, the *Agincourt* was destroyed, sending debris across the surface of the icy moon, Europa.

CHAPTER FOUR

On board the one-thousand-and-two-hundred meter-long heavy battlecruiser *Behemoth Ascending*, Third Commander Dracko was visualizing the tactical information displayed on the viewscreens. It showed that the fourth planet had only a dozen patrol ships lightly armed and a few ground energy cannons on the surface. Life sensors indicated that the population had evacuated into underground bunkers – easy targets with the new nukes they carried aboard.

Before arriving at Mars, the massive battlecruiser nuked mining outposts in the asteroid belt. After destroying the Vegan freighter, High Commander Enki ordered a thorough search of all moons and planetoids between Jupiter and Mars. Ceres was bombarded, annihilating all the posts on its surface. Destroying all signs of a Starhuman civilization was vital.

With narrowed eyes, Sensor Officer Uzug turned his gaze toward Third Commander Dracko. His expression showed concern. "Third Commander! More than a hundred fighters are in space, rapidly approaching our fleet! We didn't detect them all!"

The battlecarrier *Ascendant Ripper* possessed more than two hundred and fifty *Raptor* fighters and fifty small precision *Tyrannous* bombers. It would be an easy job to ensure that none of the Vegans fighters made it back.

Dracko nodded, drawing in a sharp breath. "Krigi, launch the fighters and attack the enemy ones. After that, send the bombers to target the dome cities, infrastructure and telecommunications. I don't want any of those civilians surviving the attack. Place some cluster tactical nukes in those damn cannons," he said in a deep, raspy voice. His yellow reptilian eyes turned red, showing no mercy.

After touching several icons, Tactical Officer Krigi sent the orders. "Fighters and bombers launching, Third Commander. Combat range in eight minutes. Two minutes for nukes. Locating cannons now," he reported, his claws touching the semi-circular holographic display in front of him. It showed red icons for enemies and green icons for friendly forces.

Third Commander Dracko was of Thuban-Ciakar descent – an aberration, according to Empress Ishtar, who vied for purity in the races. Thubans didn't believe in such a thing; they were always trying to improve their species using genetic manipulation. He had the skills for scavenging and pirating of all Thubans but the ferocity and ambition of the inhabitants of Ciakar, capital of the Draconian Empire. He had a powerful tail, lethal in CQC, which was one of the gifts he'd inherited through his Ciakan blood.

"Are we sending ground troops, Third Commander?" asked First Officer Anamesh.

Anamesh was a warrior caste, and he was impatient to rip apart some humans. The warrior caste on board the *Behemoth Ascending* also had long, lethal tails, added by genetic manipulation. It was a key advantage in close-quarter combat, making these Thuban warriors a deadly war machine. However, it was not the only benefit; he was wearing his battle armor vacuum suit, a powerful device that enhanced strength by two hundred percent. It was impervious to most known weapons.

"In time, Anamesh, at the appointed time. Let's not precipitate with the Vegans. They always seem to have some hidden assets," Dracko replied, knowing the strong officer was already tasting human blood in his mouth.

All Draconians were, to some extent, addicted to human blood. They found the taste of it very exquisite.

Most important of all, human hormones like adrenaline and cortisone made all of them high. These products were in high demand in the *butcher houses* across the empire.

-

In the situation room in the Atlantean Government Palace, Commodore Valentis watched the latest reports with concern. "*Agincourt* destroyed," he reported, not showing interest. He was sure of that outcome.

"Twenty-three enemy ships attacked some cargo ships transporting raw materials to Mars and nuked our mine outpost on Ceres," reported Sensor Operator Allumin, fear in his eyes and drops of sweat falling on the holographic command table. "They've set course for Terra, and they're almost within engaging range of our small fleet near Luna."

Atlas nodded, his gaze again lost in the shrews. "Set all units on maximum alert and prepare to engage in combat. We must save this planet and all its inhabitants. We must not perish, as this is our home now," said Consul Atlas firmly, gazing at every member of the security cabinet. Their forces were not as great as the enemy's, even if their technology was superior, but after all, they weren't a strong race and at this moment they were a very complacent one. "Order our fleet to engage the enemy in testing their weapons and pulling back to the defense grid. Activate the Goliath cannons on Luna."

"With all due respect, because you and your cronies didn't approve the cannons project for Luna, our base there is defenseless," Valentis said, attempting to make them realize how foolish they'd been in the past.

"We never thought we could use them one day," Senator Tyron said, defending the position of the cabinet for the past century. "They're expensive!"

"Now all of you will taste how sour it is to lose all your possessions and wealth," Valentis answered, gazing angrily at the greedy Senator.

"Orders sent," Comm officer Nara reported.

Commodore Valentis was aware of the Consul's daughter's service in the six-hundred-meter-long destroyer, *Blaze of Glory*. She was a beautiful Admiral, young according to the fleet's standards, but she was the Consul's daughter and that kind of relationship had its advantages. She was the acting Admiral in charge of the fleet, as the actual Fleet Admiral was in Syrius A, helping protect their allies, the Syrians, from pirates. He knew that if his daughter was to engage the enemy, she would never come back home.

-

On the south side of Olympus Mons, inside one of the six-kilometer-high cliffs, a secret hangar guarded two hundred new *Wasp* fighters, equipped with an energy screen, two tactical ten-megaton war-heads and laser cannons. They were deadly and very fast, equipped with an anti-gravity and anti-inertia drive. Pilots could turn one-hundred-and-eighty degrees in an instant, defying all physical laws.

Captain Masan checked all the systems of his fighter, *Lady Killer*. He had been a pilot for over ten years, flying all over the Solaris System. Just a few weeks earlier, he had been involved in war games in the asteroid belt against different squadrons from Terra, Mars and Ceres. He'd gotten the highest score in shooting down small asteroids and in combat simulations, which all units participated in. Masan was one hell of a fighter pilot; there were no better pilots on the whole planet. This didn't mean the other pilots were bad or less competent, but Masan stood above the rest.

"Next time I'll beat you, Masan!" Captain Gaen said in a mocking voice. They weren't close friends but rivals. Competition between pilots was a good thing because they were always trying to improve and be better at what they did. "Last time, you were lucky. If it hadn't been for that debris field you left in my way, I would have beaten you, no doubt about it!"

"You flew very well, Gaen. No doubt you could beat me. Everyone could because we're the best at this," said Masan, trying not to fall into Gaen's games of polemic and conflict. "Keep up the hard work, mate."

"We'll see each other up there next week," Gaen added, pointing at Masan.

"Sure, see you there," Masan replied, continuing his task.

Suddenly, the alarms sounded. Red lights flashed all over the hangar. "All pilots, to your combat fighters. All pilots report immediately to your combat fighters. This is not a drill. Enemy inbound," said a voice through the communication speakers. The message repeated for several minutes.

"What the hell is going on?" Gaen asked in a worried voice as he ran to his fighter, just a few meters from Masan's.

Masan was quiet. He wondered what was going on. "Enemy inbound? What enemy?" he thought.

Only one option was feasible; the *Anunnaki*, as he referred to the Thubans, were back.

-

Fleet Commodore Toldax appeared at the hangar to address the pilots. He walked firmly but with a somber gaze. "Everyone, attention!" All the pilots squared at him. "At ease. We have one Thuban battlecarrier, a battlecruiser and three escort cruisers inbound and almost within combat range of our orbital defenses. We have no fleet to defend our world; the few ships we have are aiding the Syrians against pirates. Just four destroyers are orbiting Terra at this moment to engage a superior force. The enemy outnumbers us four to one."

"We can beat those goddamn lizards again!" Gaen exclaimed.

"Yeah, we can kill them all," said the others with excited cheers.

Commodore Toldax took a deep breath. "This fleet is not like the one our ancestors fought. This one is a fully updated and powerful Draconian battle fleet. The Thubans spent every single credit they got over four hundred years to develop new technologies and weapons. I fear this time the outcome may be different."

"What are our orders, sir?" Masan asked, stopping the cheers in the hangar.

The Fleet Commodore looked up Masan; he held the Captain in high esteem. "More than a hundred old fighters from our orbital space station are already in combat range with the enemy. Our mission is to give them more firepower and to defend the station at all costs." Toldax bent his head and touched his eyes. "Many of you will die today but remember, this is our world! We have red dust in our blood! Let's make it worthwhile to be a Martian!"

Cheers and jubilation sparked all over the place. Pilots held up their helmets and shouted.

Masan remained quiet. He knew the Draconians were a confederation of many clans and factions. The most powerful were always fighting the Lyrans and other humanoid races in a far sector of the galaxy. However, the Thubans were scavengers, preying on primitive worlds to obtain a quick reward. They never found an enemy that would stand up to them in this part of the galaxy, closer to their homeworld. Masan's people had found Terra by mistake. They had been looking for a suitable world after their home planet, Atlantea, where their culture had prospered for over five thousand years at peace in the Helix System, had been destroyed because its sun had entered a supernova phase. Atlanteans were still investigating the cause of that catastrophe, as the Helix star shouldn't have become a supernova for the next three or four billion years. The only clue they had was a huge black sphere that a solar satellite had spotted. It did look artificial, but the size of that object was a quarter that of the star. Then they thought it had to be a neutron star or an errant dark matter object that impacted the sun. It was a catastrophe with no warning. Just a few hundred thousand people were evacuated, most of them fleet personnel. The fleet then joined a Lyran tactical group that heard the SOS transmissions. The Lyrans investigated whether the Draconians had settled in some worlds of this spiral arm of the galaxy. They found Terra and the planet had sentient hominids, star seeds of the ancient race that had seeded the Lyrans and all other humanoid races of the galaxy, perhaps of the universe.

"Let's do this," Masan said with conviction, knowing he might be facing his death.

Acting immediately, everyone began boarding their aircraft, some with worry on their faces, others saying, "Yeah, let's kill those goddamn salamanders!"

It was a mix of feelings. No one had been in real combat before. This battle would be their first – and perhaps their last.

-

Taloo was in his fighter, doing a routine patrol over the ocean between Poseidonia, Atlantis and the eastern peninsula. Though the Atlanteans had had no enemies in this colony world for a few centuries, some exercises were still done to maintain practice in the military arts. However, enemies lurked in every corner of the galaxy, in particular the Thubans or the Anunnaki, as the Terrans knew them, who left Solaris after a brief battle. His mission was to determine, by taking scans and photos, how human settlements could be impacted in the coastal area of the eastern continents, as ice caps were slowly retreating. He thought about what to do when he returned home to his wife and son. Taloo was looking forward to those few days of rest that he would enjoy after his duty today.

Suddenly, flashing red lights appeared as the alarm of his console activated. A voice began speaking through communications.

"Command Control to all units, I repeat, Command Control to all units, enemy detected in Solaris System, I repeat, enemy inbound."

"Here, Captain Taloo, what enemy?" he replied, concerned.

"Thubans," replied Command Control in a worried voice.

"They're back," said Captain Taloo in a low voice, trying to hide his concern. He had never been in combat before, just a few combat simulations and hundreds of hours in the air. Now the enemy was back, and they would do anything to gain control of the planet. "What are my orders, Command Control?" he asked while reducing speed until the fighter remained still over the blue ocean.

"Remain in the air and wait. You will get instructions promptly."

CHAPTER FIVE

Iigh Commander Enki of the Thuban Clan, a minor clan of the Draconian Empire, stood in the Command and Control Center of his battleship, the *Thuban Executor*, looking, in his viewscreen, at the blue-white globe he had to reconquer. It was a spine nailed into his cold heart, and he had to heal it. It was a great dishonor to have lost that planet in the past to a Starhuman race.

Draconians believed that humans were inferior beings and that this was the way it had to be. Enki also had plans for some reptilian species of that planet to become part of his clan after genetic engineering. He had studied the planet's past to discover that truly enormous reptilians were walking the surface of this world, some of them in the path of intelligence. One of those species, a raptor one, could communicate with the others of its group and set up traps or ambushes. Mysteriously, they abruptly disappeared over sixty-five million years earlier, according to his scientist caste, due to an asteroid.

"If we exterminate the humans and mammals of this world once and forever, we can bring back some extinguished species that once inhabited this planet. We could adopt some of their characteristics so that our species becomes the most powerful one in the galaxy," Second Commander Marduk said excitedly. "We do not need slaves from this world, as we have others. We must exterminate every single human to set an example."

"Perhaps you're right," answered Enki. "The fossils we found were amazing and adapting those characteristics to our race would be wise and prudent. Remember, to the Ciakans, we're just a minor clan and dispensable. They won't hesitate to exterminate us if we keep disappointing them." Enki wore a fearful look. He could already see the future awaiting him if they could complete all the plans he had in mind.

"That's true, though we may exploit every resource and spoil every survivor before we begin with our plan," Marduk said.

"Yes," commented Enki. "We will take all valuables and humans off the planet first. We may even settle them in one of our slaves' off-worlds so that we have enough food and labor. Also, the *Grays* are interested in trading some humans with us for unknown reasons."

"I hate the *Grays*. They're always so reserved," muttered Marduk.

The *Grays* were big players in galaxy affairs. They barely entered combat with anyone, but they would certainly do so if necessary, to devastating effect. For eons, Draconians had been filing complaints against the Grays for meddling in Draconian space to abduct their slaves.

"High Commander, we may have a problem," said Sensor Officer Okyd.

"What now?" Enki shouted; Okyd had caused all his plans to vanish from his mind.

"Four Vegan Destroyers are advancing toward us. The sensor scan says they're heavily armed," said Okyd.

Second Officer Ynnie lifted his head from his viewscreen and asked, "What are your orders, High Commander? If we let them attack first, we may suffer much damage."

"Get into combat range and annihilate those damn primates," Enki grunted angrily.

-

On board the six-hundred-meter-long Atlantean destroyer *Blaze of Glory*, Admiral Eve sat in her command chair in the middle of the Command Center. She was in her fifties, but that age to an Atlantean woman was similar to the twenties to a Terran one. She was over six feet tall and had tanned skin, dark hair and very dark eyes. Her father, Consul Atlas, had ordered her to attack and destroy the Thuban fleet. It was a difficult task, but it was also the only hope of retaining control of Solaris. The other part of the fleet was in a nearby system, Sirius A, assisting the Syrians, as pirates had plundered the planet. Pirates were a constant threat in the civilized galactic regions of space. Sometimes, as in this case, the pirates were humanoid.

"Status of the enemy forces?" Eve asked. She was worried, but her face showed nothing but confidence. It was her job to look serene and poised in victory. It was the way of every admiral in the fleet.

"Enemy forces formed two battle fleets. One is heading toward us and the smaller one to Mars. The first fleet consists of three battleships, seven battlecruisers, one battlecarrier and seven light escort cruisers. The second fleet over Mars consists of one battlecruiser, one battlecarrier, and three light escort cruisers," reported Captain Gadom, XO of the *Blaze of Glory*. The enemy severely outnumbered them, and this fleet was in firepower, comparable to one of the significant Draconian clans.

A cold chill ran across Eve's body. With those numbers, they didn't stand a chance. Her strategy was simple: test the enemy's weapons and energy screens, if they possessed them, and return to the small defense grid around the planet. A few assets were waiting for the Thubans. "Sensors?" she asked.

"We're almost in combat range, Admiral. Two more minutes for long-range weapons to be in optimal combat range," said Sensor Officer Solux. "Energy shields are up and everyone is ready in their battle stations."

"Prepare hyper-missiles. Target the battlecarrier and light cruisers. If we take them down first, we may be able to push them to retreat," Eve said. There was a small chance of that happening. The Draconians rarely retreated in combat, as it was a great dishonor for them to do so. However, these were the scavengers – Thubans, the lower clan in the Empire.

"Targets locked, firing hyper-missiles in twenty seconds," said Tactical Officer Coram while he pressed icons on his tactical display.

The hyper-missiles were a new development in weaponry. The missiles had a small FTL drive and, once fired, they entered hyperspace at a tremendous speed to explode in their targets microseconds after being shot.

"Fleet in combat range and combat condition," said Captain Gadom.

"Hyper-missiles loaded and ready to fire," reported Tactical Officer Coram.

"Fire them," Admiral Eve said with an evil grin on her face.

The battle for Solaris had begun.

-

The destroyers *Valorous* and *Courageous* rapidly closed formation. Their missile tubes slid open, firing their deadly payload at their target, the Thuban battlecarrier. Eight hyper-missiles fired and vanished in hyperspace only to reappear a microsecond later, targeting the reptilian vessel. Huge explosions suddenly lit up space. Once the energy dispersed, the battlecarrier still held its position, but it had suffered damage from the blast. One or perhaps two additional well-placed missiles and the ship could have vanished.

From the destroyer *Blaze of Glory*, missile tubes slid open and four hyper-missiles exited them to vanish in hyperspace. Microseconds later, the fifty-megaton anti-matter missiles impacted their targets, two of the escort cruisers. Nova-like explosions were visible in the enemy cruisers. The enemy's energy screen seemed to glow due to the tremendous amount of energy that the deadly missiles had released. In a moment, the screens appeared to hold, but two of the seven light cruisers exploded, sending debris in all directions.

The destroyer *Adventurer* closed position on an enemy cruiser in a daring maneuver and fired its deadly missiles. The enemy cruiser turned to avoid impact, but it couldn't see the inbound missiles until they exploded against the energy shield, making it glow in a ball of anti-matter fire. The screen couldn't resist the amount of energy released against it and seemed to flicker. The antimatter fire found a weakness in the shield, penetrated the hull and tore it apart, cutting through the rear bulkhead of the vessel. A moment later, the Thuban escort cruiser exploded, leaving behind a ball of glowing gas.

-

"Three light cruisers down. Battlecarrier still operative but severely damaged," reported an excited Sensor Officer Solux.

"Twenty seconds until the next barrage of hyper-missiles," Tactical Officer Coram said.

"Target locks and fire energy beams and lasers," Admiral Eve ordered. She had achieved the first success, but all the enemy's battleships and battlecruisers kept moving forward.

-

The six-hundred-meter-long destroyer *Adventurer* fired its cannon beams and energy projectors against an enemy battleship. It was a daring maneuver, as the battleship could quickly destroy the Atlantean ship, but it seemed that the Thubans were in shock after the hyper-missile attack. Energy beams and energy projectors impacted the battleship. Energy screens seemed to hold when the second barrage of hyper-missiles left the tubes of the destroyer. Moments later, the missiles hit when more energy beams and projectors fired in the same location as the rockets. Antimatter energy glowed in a ferocious fireball, like a supernova, when the beams penetrated the thick hull of the battleship. Once the antimatter energy dissipated, the Thuban battleship began drifting powerlessly in space. Seconds later, more energy beams and projectors tore apart the ship, which exploded. A debris field impacted the Thuban flagship, the *Thuban Executor.*

-

The *Thuban Executor* shook violently after the explosions surrounded it. High Commander Enki was almost thrown from his command chair. It had been a wise decision to sit instead of stand, as he often did. "What was that?" he asked in shock.

"A type of missile with antimatter warheads, High Commander," Second Commander Marduk reported.

"Antimatter?" Enki asked in disbelief.

The Vegans had never shown such weapons in the past, and it was a dangerous development. Draconians had such weapons but not his clan. They were very expensive and, to avoid civil conflicts in the empire, neither the High Draconian Council nor the Empress allowed lesser groups to use such massively destructive weapons. Every clan wanted more power in the empire hierarchy, and Enki knew everything about that. His plan was for his family to become the ruling one, with himself named Emperor.

"Antimatter in the fifty-megaton range, but the missiles are so fast, we can't stop them before they hit us," replied Marduk in a frightened voice. Enki had never seen Marduk afraid of anything, except for upsetting him. As Second Commander, he couldn't disappoint a High Commander, as the consequences of doing so were severe, including the death penalty.

"Losses?" Enki asked fearfully.

Marduk checked the tactical display and felt a chill cross his body. "We lost three escort cruisers and the battleship *Starbutcher*. The battlecarrier *Blood Fury* is severely damaged but operative."

Enki's face turned pale. "Fire everything we've got upon them!" he ordered in desperation.

It was vital to destroy those few Vegan ships as fast as possible. If the Vegans placed a few of those missiles in his battleships, the results could be devastating, as the *Starbutcher* was identical to the *Thuban Executor* in weapons and shields.

-

From the Draconian fleet, missile tubes slid opened and fifty-megaton nuclear warheads left at high speed toward the enemy destroyers. Dozens of missiles were visible when Vegan railguns opened fire, intercepting most of them. Slightly more than ten of them impacted their targets. A nova-like explosion appeared in two of the Vegan destroyers. After the nuclear fire dispersed, one destroyer, the *Courageous*, remained intact and continued its advance, while the *Adventurer*, the closest in combat to the reptilian fleet, blew apart in a brilliant flash of light, sending debris in all directions.

The battleship *Thuban Executor* and the *Dog of War*, combining fire with the rest of the battlecruisers, let loose their cannon beams, energy projectors and ion and particle beams, seeking any breach in the Vegans' energy screens.

-

In the Command Center of the Atlantean destroyer *Blaze of Glory*, Admiral Eve was in shock as she saw the *Adventurer* blow apart. Even before the battle began, it had been evident that they would die that day. She had known most of the crew of that ship for years. Now they were all gone. At least they knew they could beat a Thuban battleship.

"Destroyer *Adventurer* down!" Sensor Officer Solux reported in a frightened voice. Sweat was running down his face as he turned pale. "The enemy is firing more energy weapons! Impact in five seconds!"

"Energy screens holding at seventy-five percent," added Captain Gadom in a frantic voice, knowing they had only a few seconds of life left.

"Move us out of here!" Admiral Eve ordered, struggling to stay calm.

-

In space, white, bright orange and dark blue beams were inbound to the remaining Vegan fleet. This one, in a move of desperation, changed course but it was too late. Beam after beam impacted the destroyers' energy screens violently. The destroyers *Valorous* and *Courageous* couldn't resist the huge amount of energy fired upon them after the first barrage of nuclear power when an energy beam penetrated the screen of the *Valorous*, tearing apart the engineering deck. Huge holes in the hull of the ship were visible and other energy and ion beams penetrated the vessel's thick armor. At that moment, the *Valorous* blew apart as the antimatter reactor overloaded and exploded. A brilliant nova, like a miniature sun, seemed to disappear moments later, leaving behind a glowing ball of gas and wreckage.

The *Courageous* held for a few more seconds, drifting powerlessly in space. Then particle beams fired from every significant Thuban vessel and it suffered dozens of impacts in its hull. Moments later, it also blew apart.

Only the *Blaze of Glory* remained spared but heavily damaged.

-

Admiral Eve was semi-conscious on top of her destroyed tactical display. The last attack had heavily damaged most of the compartments of the vessel. In the Command Center, a few bodies were lifeless in their combat stations. Most of the tactical displays and viewscreens were damaged. Small fires raged on top of every station. Eve opened her eyes to realize that she was alive, but not for long.

"Status?" asked the Admiral in a low and pained voice. She was coughing, as the ventilation system seemed to have stopped working and smoke was rapidly filling the whole place. No one replied to her question. She turned her face in a painful movement and saw Captain Gadom sitting in his chair. He was dead. His face appeared disfigured and blood was puddling under his chair. Eve suddenly erupted into tears as she saw, beside Captain Gadom, her Sensor Officer lying still on the metallic deck's floor. A piece of metal had cut Solux across his chest. She hoped he had died fast and hadn't felt anything.

Everything was lost.

Tactical Officer Coram was injured, though he managed to talk. "Admiral," he said, coughing. "Energy screens offline. Weapons systems offline. Heavy damage in engineering and sectors five, seven, ten and fourteen. Sub-light and FTL drive offline. Life support at fifteen percent and rapidly decreasing." His coughing worsened and he spat blood.

Eve turned her face toward him to see that he had just died with his eyes riveted on her. It was a grievous situation. All her friends on that ship were dead. The *Blaze of Glory* would be remembered, if anyone survived this war, as the *Embracer of Death*.

Eve had to do one more thing: Send a message to her father, Consul Atlas. She pressed her comm icon in one of the displays that partially worked. "Here, Admiral Eve of the *Blaze of Glory*. Mission failed. The destroyers *Courageous*, *Valorous* and *Adventurer* are destroyed. All our systems have failed. We're powerless in space." She paused for a moment when tears began to run down her cheeks. All her memories crossed her mind at a tremendous speed. "Dad, I'm sorry. I have failed you and our people. Tell Mum I love her so much as I love you..."

Suddenly, an energy beam filled the Command Center with bright, white light. Moments later, the *Blaze of Glory* exploded, killing everyone on board.

-

"Enemy ships destroyed," said Second Commander Marduk as the last red threat icon disappeared from his tactical display.

"Very well. Continue our advance to the planet. Launch the fighters and bombers. Order them to destroy the defense satellites and platforms," said High Commander Enki, grinning.

He was closer to reconquering the gold planet, as he always referred to Terra. This time he would exterminate the Vegans and most of the native population. Only a few thousand would survive the genocide he was about to commit, and their survival would be for one reason: to extract as much gold as possible. He would make sure the surviving humans died working in the mines, and those who might survive would settle another slave off-world.

More than one hundred defensive satellites orbiting the planet began firing at the Thuban fleet with their dual-energy cannon. The sixteen defense platforms armed with Goliath cannons followed.

"Enemy satellites are opening fire," reported Sensor Officer Okyd as a small red icon appeared on the screen. "Fighters are engaging the satellites and bombers are targeting the platforms with tactical nuclear warheads."

"Prepare the ground troops' shuttles. We are to begin the invasion," ordered High Commander Enki.

"As you command," said First Officer Ebagesh, quickly leaving the Command Center.

CHAPTER SIX

Several minutes passed in the situation room at the Atlantean Government Palace, situated in the central concentric ring of Atlantis. The movement inside was very chaotic. In a holographic display in the middle of the situation table station, the progress of the current battle between the Atlantean and Thuban fleets was showing a catastrophic outcome; the Atlanteans were on the losing end.

"We lost three destroyers!" Sensor Operator Allumin exclaimed, his face turning pale.

Consul Atlas' heart suddenly stopped. "What's the status of the *Blaze of Glory*?"

Valentis interrupted, as it was better that he deliver the news. "The *Blaze of Glory* is powerless, drifting in space, Consul." Valentis suddenly looked at the communications display as he received a message. "Message incoming!"

"Play it on the viewscreen," ordered Atlas, hoping it was from his daughter.

Valentis pressed an icon and the image of the young Admiral appeared. Everyone was still watching the message from Admiral Eve, covered with bruises and blood, when a white light abruptly ended it.

A sudden silence covered the place as the green icon of the *Blaze of Glory*, the Consul's daughter's ship, disappeared from the holographic viewscreen.

Like everyone else, Consul Atlas remained quiet for several minutes. No one dared say anything, as the pain the Consul felt in that moment was the greatest ever imagined for a human being: losing a child. Tears ran down the Consul's face; then he crumbled. It was too much. Losing his only daughter in that cruel manner, thousands of fleet personnel dead and, once again, at the brink of losing another homeworld.

His tears stopped and the Consul stood again with a severe gaze. "Make them pay," he said, revenge in his eyes.

"They're here!" screamed Sensor Operator Allumin. "They're engaged with our orbital defenses."

"Damn it," said Commodore Valentis. "Send all fighters and bombers to the outer atmosphere and shoot the Goliath Cannons!"

The Goliath Cannons were the Atlanteans' ultimate defensive weapon. They were eighty-meter-high double energy cannons that shot an energy beam capable of reaching outer space to a maximum altitude of forty-thousand kilometers. Twenty of them were located across the planet.

"Air force in combat, cannons are shooting, Commodore," said Allumin with visible tension in his body. The first of the cannons shot the double white energy beam, which, in just a couple of seconds, impacted an enemy battleship at twenty-eight thousand kilometers. However, it didn't have the expected effect. "Cannons ineffective, sir."

Four hundred years earlier, when the battle for Terra occurred, the Draconian Thubans, or Anunnaki, didn't possess any energy screen. However, the Vegans did have one, giving them the ultimate strategic advantage in the battle. It was a decisive factor in the Vegans' victory, as they destroyed Thuban ships with impunity.

"Impossible!" Consul Atlas shouted furiously, dissipating all hope for a victory.

"They must have developed a powerful Draconian energy shield, which is why they did not come back," said Valentis in despair. He recriminated the greedy and fooled Consul: "The cannons are designed to destroy missiles inbound against the surface of ships with shields weaker than ours. Again, proof of your incompetence. Your greed will lead us to defeat!" Atlanteans had become greedy over time, as people lost their vitality and dreams.

"We are doomed," Atlas declared, bowing his head in surrender. "Evacuate everyone. All military personnel, government and civilians to the shuttles."

"But sir, there aren't enough shuttles for everyone," Valentis said, his face showing a growing concern.

"I know. Evacuate as many people as possible and leave. Now!" shouted the Consul in anger. "Deploy combat robots. Let's make them pay with blood!"

-

Captain Taloo was ascending with a squadron of fifteen fighters, armed with energy cannons and two ten-kiloton warheads for use in extreme situations. These vessels weren't the modern *Wasp* fighters that were deployed at Mars, as their production had started only a year earlier.

The squadron was over twenty thousand kilometers high when they located the enemy ships, just slightly over eight thousand kilometers away.

"We have visual contact with the enemy," Taloo said through his comm channel. "Five minutes for combat range. Squadron in combat formation."

No one replied from the Command and Control Center. Taloo's concern grew. He re-sent the message, but nothing came back. It was like they had simply left. A third attempt to establish communication with the Command and Control Center was made, with identical results.

"What's going on, Captain? Why is no one answering down there?" asked Lieutenant Durro. The lieutenant was over five hundred meters away from Taloo's fighter.

"I don't know, Lieutenant. Perhaps it's a security measure – you know, black out all communications in an attempt to avoid a nuke," Taloo replied, not convinced of what he had just said. He had to remain calm; his squadron's survival depended on that. "Let's get those sons of bitches."

"Yeah, let's get those goddamn salamanders," said other pilots animatedly through communications.

-

Minutes passed rapidly and the fifteen-fighter squadron entered combat range.

In space, thirty nuclear warheads, in the ten-kiloton range, fired against the Thuban battleships and battlecruisers, two missiles at each enemy vessel. Taloo's squadron spared the escort cruisers for the time being, instead attempting to destroy the bigger ships. Perhaps the Goliath cannons could finish the work with the smaller ones.

Railguns fired from the Thuban ships, intercepting almost every inbound missile. Only two missiles impacted the enemy battleship, *Dog of War*. Brilliant flashes of nuclear fire erupted, making the battleship's energy screen glow. Once the energy had dissipated, the vessel remained unharmed.

Taloo was in shock, as he didn't know the enemy possessed energy screens. In the flight academy, when they had studied the first battle against the Thubans in which Commodore Toldax had commanded the Atlantean battleship *Atlantis Pioneer*, he had always been told that Thubans were so inferior in technology, they hadn't developed energy screens. That wasn't true. Thubans were scavengers, always preying on lesser civilizations, most of them of agrarian and without a chance of resisting them; therefore, the need for energy screens was secondary. Draconians did have energy screens; their shields were among the most powerful in the galaxy. However, only the most prominent clans used them, as they were always at war against other humanoids and alien civilizations.

After the nuclear attack, numerous semi-circular vessels left the enemy battlecarrier. Promptly, the fireworks show began. Energy beams and lasers were everywhere. The semi-circular Thuban fighters did not possess an energy screen, which was an advantage for the Atlantean opponents that did have one. However, they were severely outnumbered, twenty to one.

Taloo saw a red light blinking in his console. It indicated a locked target. He felt a chill cross his body as he saw, in his viewscreen, the onslaught of enemy fighters leaving the battlecarrier. Without hesitation, he pressed the firing button. The flashing target locked in his holographic cockpit panel disappeared as two energy beams were shot from his wing's cannons. They made short work of the enemy vessel, which instantly became a fireball.

"Enemy vessel down!" Taloo said through his comm channel. "Next target locked." He fired and another vessel was down. "One more!" he said excitedly.

In a moment, everything changed. Battlecruisers opened fire from their railguns and laser turrets. One by one, over half the Atlantean fighters were shot down. Without the support of the destroyers, the Atlanteans had no real chance of victory. There was no hope, but it was the right thing to do, fighting for one's people and one's home. Taloo would die a hero.

Taloo was doing evasive maneuvers to skip the massive attack from some enemy vessels and one battlecruiser when Lieutenant Durro spoke. "Enemy fighters surround me; my energy screen is down to thirty percent. I won't stand another hit!"

Taloo tried to respond but Lieutenant Durro's green icon vanished from the viewscreen.

Still concentrating on evading the enemy fire, he realized that he was the only pilot left in combat. A sudden feeling of defeat crossed his heart. Taloo changed course in a daring maneuver, accelerating his fighter and momentarily leaving the battle. Then, he sought the nearest enemy vessel. He quickly calculated the power of those energy shields and made the capital decision to ram a battlecruiser. Atlanteans' old fighters couldn't maneuver as the *Wasp* ones, but they were very fast. If he could accelerate up to twenty percent the speed of light, sixty thousand meters a second, he could cut through the enemy screen. The fighter had the anti-inertia drive; hence, he would be alive at the moment of impact. He thought one more time about his wife and son; he wished to see them again. Then he accelerated his fighter, diverting all energy to the drive. Taloo spoke the motto of his squadron: "Honor and Glory." Those were his last words.

-

Taloo's fighter became almost a beam of light when, suddenly, it cut through the energy screen of the Draconian battlecruiser *Scorpion*, ramming the ship's sublight and FTL drives. A massive explosion shook the rear side of the Thuban formation. A huge nova-like explosion destroyed the battlecruiser, sending debris in all directions. Once the energy cleared, all that was left was a glowing ball of gas and wreckage.

-

On board the *Thuban Executor*, High Commander Enki watched in disbelief as the battlecruiser *Scorpion* vanished from the viewscreen. Suddenly, the ship shook violently as pieces of wreckage from the twelve-hundred-meter-long ship impacted the shields.

"What was that?" Enki demanded from the metal ground of the Command Center. He was thrown to the floor, where he hit his head.

"An enemy fighter accelerated to twenty percent the speed of light and rammed the *Scorpion*'s drives. Our energy shields are not designed to stop something at that speed," Second Commander Marduk explained as he spat a few of his sharp and reptile fangs, which were covered in dark purple blood.

"Damn!" Enki shouted, frowning in wrath.

If a few more human pilots thought about ramming in that way, most of his fleet would be destroyed.

"All enemy fighters are down. Bombers eliminated the defense satellites during the battle and the ground-based cannons are being nuked at this moment, High Commander," reported Marduk, still spitting blood.

"Begin the invasion. We need to acquire some of the technology the Vegans use. After that, nuke all native settlements," ordered High Commander Enki angrily.

"We will become very powerful, one of the most powerful in the galaxy, if we get some of their technology," said Marduk, trying to cheer up the High Commander.

"Ground troop shuttles are on their way," Second Officer Ynnie reported. "Twenty minutes for landing."

CHAPTER SEVEN

Captain Masan was in his fighter, the *Lady Killer*, in the outer Martian atmosphere. He was the second in charge of the attack against the five Thuban warships, just behind Commodore Toldax. It was a surprise that the Commodore had taken a fighter and joined the fight against the lizards.

They had just received the bad news about Terra and the small fleet defending the planet. Now it was clear that they were the last Atlantean bastion to stop this cruel invasion. More than one hundred old fighters were already engaging with the enemy fleet, causing heavy damage to the enemy's fighters and bombers. The light escort cruisers were suffering, trying to track and shoot them down, though a few well-placed nukes did impact the surface of the planet. The fighter's primary mission was to intercept the inbound missiles targeting the red globe. That wasn't the case, as someone had made a colossal mistake. The Goliath cannons were unable to shoot down all nukes, and the railgun batteries were unfinished – and, therefore, useless in this battle.

The domed city of *Agartha*, the capital city of Mars, was destroyed. Just the pyramid complex and the human face, made of enormous stone blocks, survived. Other small towns, such as *Triton* and *Cepheus*, in the equatorial and south regions of the planet were also annihilated as nuclear fire destroyed their energy shields. Luckily, they didn't target the *Titan Project*, as it was deep below the surface. The results could be catastrophic if the enemy knew about that place; fortunately, the enemy didn't show signs of having that knowledge. Some city survivors traveled in a deep underground transport system of maglevs. More than ten thousand survivors were now safe in the Titan Complex, over two thousand meters below the surface at *Mariner Valley*. Atlanteans had chosen that area for the project because the crust of the planet was thinner there than in other locations, making it the perfect place to build the colossal megastructure.

Some shuttles left the planet as had happened at Terra, although their destination was unknown. Perhaps a few thousand would settle somewhere else. The most logical target was *Sirius A*, as the other ten warships of the Atlantean fleet were there. There was hope, but in the Solaris System, there was only death and misery.

"Two minutes for combat range. All squadrons to target enemy fighters and bombers. After that, everyone to target the battlecruiser drives in a synchronized attack with nukes in the same area of the enemy ships within the millisecond. That might work," Commodore Toldax said through his comm.

"Roger that, *Wasp* two," Captain Masan replied.

Acting immediately, two hundred *Wasp* fighters replied in unison.

"Good luck and good hunting," Toldax added confidently.

He started accelerating, as he was free of the Martian atmosphere. The battle between the old *Dragon* fighters and the Draconian Thubans was almost over, and more news from Terra had just come in; the planet fell silent, indicating that it had fallen to enemy forces. Only the four-thousand-meter station was standing in the Martian orbit. The enemy hadn't shown an interest in destroying the station yet; perhaps they had plans for it in the future. The station had an energy screen, but it was unarmed. That was a terrible mistake. That station could have the same firepower as ten Atlantean battleships, as the antimatter reactors that were used to power it were more than capable of supporting several weapons systems. Again, Atlanteans weren't a strong race, and they had become too complacent. That had to change if the Atlantean race was destined to survive.

Two minutes passed and the two hundred *Wasp* fighters began their fire attack. Energy bursts illuminated space. It was a ferocious and intense battle. This time, Martian fighters outnumbered the enemy ones, as they hadn't expected the second battalion, this time better equipped and advanced, which had shown up. Now they were shooting them down.

Captain Masan was maneuvering at high G speeds, but he couldn't feel anything, as the anti-inertia drive made the small fighter defy the laws of physics. "Fourth enemy fighter down," he said in jubilation.

He kept changing direction in impossible twirls. Another enemy fighter became a fireball. This amazed him, as the Thubans had spent four centuries preparing themselves for this day and they had never thought about equipping their fighters and bombers with energy shields. That was more proof of how stingy they were about spending money. Other Draconian clans weren't like the Thubans, as their warships possessed the latest technology, but the Thubans were scavengers. A quick profit with no harm was what they always wanted, and they thrived that way.

-

On board the *Behemoth Ascending*, Third Commander Dracko was getting alarmed, as more green icons representing his fighters were disappearing from the tactical display. "What's going on?" he shouted, revealing his sharp reptile fangs covered with thick saliva. "Where are those fighters coming from and why are they moving in that way?"

"Unknown, Third Commander," replied Tactical Officer Krigi. "They must have some anti-inertia and anti-gravity drives."

"That's impossible!" Dracko spat angrily. "Shoot them down, now!"

"I have an idea, Third Commander," said Sensor Officer Yakub, getting the attention of everyone in the Command Center.

"Go ahead," replied Dracko with curiosity.

"According to a battle simulation I ran when the new enemy fighters showed up, we have an eighty-nine percent chance of surviving if we destroy the orbiting space yard," Yakub answered, expanding his calculations in the main viewscreen.

"What about the fighters? They're the problem here," Dracko responded, not understanding where the Sensor Officer was going with his theory.

Yakub swallowed and took a deep breath. "If we place a few nukes in that station, once destroyed, the expansive wave and debris will annihilate the small enemy fighters. The explosion would affect them, as an electromagnetic pulse will fry their systems. Surely, the power systems of those crafts couldn't resist such a pulse."

Third Commander Dracko remained silent for a moment, thinking about Yakub's plan. The Sensor Officer's idea was brilliant, and if he was right, the enemy wouldn't stand a chance. "What about us? Will we be affected by that pulse of yours?" Dracko couldn't afford to lose the battlecarrier or his flagship, the *Behemoth Ascending*. He had spent many *draks*, hundreds of millions of them, to make the *Behemoth* one of the most potent battlecruisers in the Empire.

"Perhaps minor damage, mostly from big chunks of metal wreckage," Yakub said, confident that his plan could work.

"Krigi, inform the fleet of our plan. Divert all available power to the energy screens. Use only missiles to target the station," Dracko ordered. Suddenly, an explosion shook the ship violently. "What was that?" he grunted.

"A nuke!" Tactical Officer Krigi exclaimed. "Energy screen holding at eighty-two percent."

Another missile struck the ship, making the screens glow in a bright ball of nuclear energy.

"Attack!" Dracko shouted in a panic.

"Fleet firing fifty-megaton warheads against the space station! Ten seconds for impact," Sensor Officer Yakub said.

-

In space, the battle between the Draconian Thubans, or Anunnaki as native Terrans knew them in Solaris System, and the surviving Atlanteans raged wildly. Captain Masan groaned when he saw multiple missile tubes slide open in the enemy vessels. Instantly, dozens of tactical nukes exited the tubes at tremendous speed. Those missiles weren't hyper-missiles, but they had a sub-light mini drive installed with a top rate of ten percent the speed of light. Masan's heart suddenly stopped as he realized where the missiles were heading: the orbital space yard, a large area four thousand meters wide, two thousand meters high and two thousand meters deep, with two construction yards and two repair bays. The station was unarmed but equipped with an energy screen. Surely, if just a few of those nukes struck the station, the battle would be over. Most of Commodore Toldax and Captain Masan's fighters were in the vicinity of the vast station to protect it. Another huge mistake.

"All fighters to intercept those missiles," Masan said through his comm unit to every pilot alive. More than one hundred and fifty *Wasp* fighters were still in combat.

Many fighters did the impossible twirls and maneuvers in space at such a speed that, in a matter of one or two seconds, they were shooting down missiles. Unfortunately, there were too many, as the Draconian vessels were emptying their tubes.

Frantically, Commodore Toldax spoke. Captain Masan already knew what the Commodore was going to say. "Retreat! Everyone get out of the blast area! Return to base!"

-

Nuke after nuke struck the structure. Bright balls of nuclear power were visible all around the station. The energy screen of the Atlantean megastructure was glowing intensely. More nukes impacted the same areas of the station screens, looking for any weakness. Then one of the *Behemoth Ascending* sub-light missiles cut through the screen and impacted the rear side of the station's thick armored hull, tearing it apart. Moments later, internal explosions occurred inside the station, annihilating the three thousand crew members aboard. A massive explosion blew it apart while more nukes arrived and detonated. With a force equivalent to that of a massive solar storm, a truly massive nova-like explosion sent an electromagnetic pulse all over Mars' orbit and the planet's surface. The fighters' power systems couldn't hold that enormous amount of released energy. Suddenly, a hundred and forty-two *Wasp* fighters remained powerless in the cold and now rapidly approaching debris field in space. Huge pieces of metal wreckage began impacting and destroying the vessels. Small explosions covered the ongoing nova that became the station.

-

Captain Masan couldn't believe what had just happened. There was no hope. He was about to die, and nothing could help him. "If there is a God out there, take me with you quickly," he muttered when a piece of wreckage over fifty meters in diameter struck his fighter, leaving behind a small explosion.

-

Commander Padis, Governor of Mars, couldn't believe what was occurring. "Terra's fleet has been destroyed. No Atlantean fighter survived. We lost everything." He shook his head in disbelief, the frown deepening on his face.

"Sir," Vera said sadly. "We can overload the Titan cannon to reach deep inside the planet. Then we could detonate a few anti-matter warheads inside the planet's core. Perhaps if we destroy this world, the Thubans will leave forever."

Padis gazed at her, struggling to stay calm. "No," he replied evenly. "That could destroy Terra as well. It's more than certain that a huge part of the planet would be captured by Terra's gravity well, as Mars is in its closest orbit. We must not make the living beings of Terra pay the consequences of our incompetence; they have the right to survive."

Vera felt deeply ashamed. "I am sorry, Commander. I am just a computer program trying to find solutions," she said, looking at the floor.

"You are more than a computer program and you know it," Padis replied affectionately. "How many people are being evacuated?"

Vera quickly checked the latest data available to her. "More than ten thousand, sir. No more survivors are coming through the maglevs. The self-destruction of the transport tunnels was activated over twelve minutes ago to prevent the enemy, which at this moment is landing in the outskirts of the nuked cities, from finding this complex."

"Ten thousand from more than a million. God help us!" Padis exclaimed, surprising Vera with his words.

She had never known the Commander was religious. Religion was a thing of the past. Vegans, like other humanoid races, didn't believe in a God, but she knew, in moments like this one, humans tended to find a mystical answer to their fears. It was in their nature, even if she couldn't understand those feelings.

"God bless us," Vera replied, extending her holographic hand and attempting to touch the Commander's shoulder, without success.

-

"All enemy fighters and the space station destroyed," Sensor Officer Yakub said with a grin on his face. Naturally, this success would result in his promotion to a better status among the fleet personnel.

"Very well," said Dracko, complacent about how the battle had gone. Small impacts were hitting the Thuban tactical force as the debris field of what had once been a large enemy orbital station passed Dracko's warships. Seconds later, the vibration of the impacts ceased and Dracko turned his reptilian face toward First Officer Anamesh. "It's your turn. Seek any survivors on the planet's surface and annihilate them. For each head you bring me, you will be rewarded with one million *draks*," said the Third Commander with a wild look on his face.

"It will be done," replied Anamesh, turning around and marching toward the shuttle's bay, where his one thousand ferocious warriors were impatiently waiting.

CHAPTER EIGHT

B ack on Terra, more than ten thousand deadly
warriors landed in strategic locations on the
planet. Over sixty percent of them were assault-
ing Poseidonia and Atlantis. The other forty percent
were capturing potential slaves among the native population and eliminating the rest. Children were spared
but captured. Their blood was a precious bounty, as
their high levels of hormones when frightened would
sell well in the *Butcher Houses* back in Thuban Prime.

Ebagesh was leading a platoon of warriors, all
equipped with deadly energy weapons and massive battle armored suits, into the city of Atlantis. They landed
the shuttles just outside the tall, white walls of the town.
To his surprise, everything seemed abandoned. He
couldn't buy that. Surely these Atlantean Vegans were
hiding and planning something.

"First Officer, the city gates are wide open," reported
Second Officer Askax.

"This doesn't feel right. What are the reports from the
surveillance drones?"

"No life detection except for this building in the center of the city," Askax said, showing Ebagesh the data on the small tactical display located in his left arm. "Perhaps the cowards evacuated and left the planet."

"Perhaps," Ebagesh said with disappointment. "Take two squads and search for hiding forces or survivors. Do not take prisoners; kill them all," he ordered.

"Will do, First Officer," replied Askax, moving inside the city walls with fifty deadly warriors.

For the next hour, they found nothing inside the city except for empty buildings and streets. Ebagesh had a growing suspicion that they had just entered an ambush. Everything indicated that. The fact that they had never faced close combat against these humans concerned him. He didn't know what kind of combat strategies the Atlantean Vegans used in close-quarter combat. It was almost unknown what weapons they might have among their military ground troops. The first time they had contacted this type of Vegan was four hundred years earlier, and they hadn't fought in that way. After the space battle, they simply annihilated the Thubans who were on the planet's surface from space or by air using the bombers and fighters, not to mention the rebellions of most of the natives' settlements.

Suddenly, the Sensor Operator's tactical display began to show movement. "First Officer, I've got something on the screen, two hundred meters north, behind those buildings." He pointed over to the place.

"Humans?" Ebagesh asked, impatient to enter combat.

"Unknown, First Officer. There is just movement, but I can't get any life sensor readings," the Sensor Operator said in confusion.

Suddenly, blue energy bursts impacted him, cutting through his thick armor as if it were butter.

"Contacts! Open fire!" Ebagesh ordered his hundred heavily armored soldiers.

"We can't see the enemy!" shouted one of the confused warriors.

"Just fire, you damn idiot!" Ebagesh said, shooting his energy weapon in the direction of the supposed enemy's location.

More energy weapons fired, killing one after another of Ebagesh's warriors in an unstoppable sequence of death. Then the enemy finally showed up. With a jump, a frightening opponent stood just a few meters away from Ebagesh. It was a combat robot.

-

Amma was doing some research in the Raman city of Andhakas, evaluating the reptilian impact on the local culture. Her mission was to gradually guide the people to a more civilized Atlantean culture without forgetting the evil ones. She knew one day the Thubans would return.

"These people always referred to the evil Ghurka; some say it's Shiva. I wonder who that lizard is," Odoc said while scanning, with his computer device, some texts in the Thuban language from a wall of the temple they were exploring that day.

Odoc was Amma's assistant and research co-worker. Both had been in the city for over a year.

"I guess he was the local governor of the city. The locals have legends about him being a perverse and odd creature. He loved to drink blood from young virgin girls," Amma said, disgusted.

Odoc gave her a startled gaze, as he hadn't known those details. "I have a bad feeling something horrible is about to happen."

"Those dreams again?" Amma asked with narrowed eyes.

"Yes, but this time I woke up with my nose bleeding and my bed full of blood. It was frightening," Odoc said, his face turning pale.

"Our people have some extra sensorial abilities, premonition being one of them. Don't worry; everything will be fine."

Suddenly, they heard screams and people running just outside the temple. Both looked at each other in confusion. "They're back! This was my dream!" Odoc said, his heart racing.

"What you talking about? No one is back!" Amma responded, trying to maintain control of her emotions.

"They're back! They're back!" Odoc continued to scream when energy weapons shot outside the temple's gate.

A young girl hurried inside the temple. Blood covered her, and she showed distress and fear.

"What's going on outside?" Amma asked the teenager in her language.

The girl gazed Amma and said, "The evil ones are back! Run if you want to live!"

Odoc began breathing rapidly. Then, in a quick movement, he ran behind the girl. Both were suddenly stopped in their march by an alien, who was waiting outside the back door.

"You can't escape, dumb human!" said the alien in a deep, raspy voice.

Amma watched in shock as Odoc took the girl and placed her behind himself. He was trying to be a hero after he had left his colleague and one of his best friends behind and alone.

"Leave her alone, you damn bastard salamander!" Odoc said, gazing at the alien defiantly. He'd made a mistake, a truly huge one; he'd spoken in the Atlantean dialect, a variant of Vegan language that the alien, in no time, had recognized.

"Vegan!" said the alien in apparent anger and surprise. Immediately, from the alien's right arm, an extensible sword appeared, sliding from the top of his hand. In a quick lurch, Odoc's head fell to the floor, his neck gushing blood like a fountain.

"No! You damn bastard!" Amma shouted in desperation, having seen her friend cruelly beheaded without a chance of defending himself.

The alien looked up at the young girl and knocked her out, leaving the body unconscious on the stone ground of the temple. Then, with a tarrying laugh, the murderer steadily walked toward Amma. He knew she was Vegan. "You are going to die slowly, Vegan. I will make sure you are alive while I dismember you."

-

Ebagesh fell on the ground to avoid a hit from the robot's metallic arm, which opened a hole in the pavement. He rolled to the side and stood to open fire with his energy rifle at the robot's head, tearing it from the rest of its body. "Die, damn machine!" he shouted, grinning at the falling robot.

All around him, more close combat occurred with worse results; many of his warriors died as the robots caught them by surprise.

Ebagesh rapidly charged against another robot. He jumped on its back, held its head with his powerful arms, powered by his combat armor, and tore apart the automat's head. "Keep fighting!" he ordered, watching as another of his warriors was shot down. He opened his communication channel in a desperate move and spoke. "Here, First Officer Ebagesh, we need reinforcements. We're fighting combat robots. No human forces detected."

"Reinforcements on the way. Pull back, orbital bombardment in one minute. I repeat, retreat five city blocks or an energy beam will catch you," said the voice statically.

"Received, we're retreating," Ebagesh replied.

CHAPTER NINE

Anamesh was leading a small platoon of warriors inside the nuked city of Agartha, the capital of Mars. Only rubble remained in the town, but he had a mission: seek, find and kill every survivor … if anyone was alive. Beside him was Ebadan, a young scientist from Ciakar. He wasn't a Ciakan, but his caste had inhabited the planet for thousands of years. Ebadan resembled a humanoid so much that Anamesh distrusted the young scientist. The scientist caste was a hybrid of reptilians and Grays. That hybridization had occurred over a million years in the past, when the Draconians had found a Gray world and destroyed it. After that, the locations of the Gray worlds were unknown. It was said across the empire that the attack against that world was the beginning of the unstoppable expansion of the Draconian Empire, as their scientist caste became super intelligent, giving the major clans of the empire the advancement they needed.

Ebadan's mission was to evaluate any technology found on the planet that could benefit the Thuban clan.

"Stay behind. I don't want to die defending your caste," Anamesh said arrogantly.

Ebadan was used to that treatment. He gazed at Anamesh and grinned. "As you wish, warrior caste. Mind your own business; I'll mind my own."

Among the ruins of the city, no survivors were visible. Without the protection of the domes, and without a vacuum suit, no human could survive longer than twenty seconds on the surface of Mars. The radiation levels were tremendous. Luckily, the invading force was protected by its powerful combat gear.

"Everything is so damn quiet. Reports all over the planet say that no survivors are left here," the comm operator said calmly.

Suddenly, an energy beam whirred and impacted one of Anamesh's warriors, beheading him. The body crashed to the dusty red ground.

"Enemy inbound, open fire!" Anamesh shouted, impatient to rip apart the humans.

More blue energy beams swept across the Thuban formation, killing more warriors. No one seemed to know who was shooting.

"No life detection, sir!" reported Sensor Operator Enoki, his expression deeply concerned.

A scream revealed the truth. "Combat robots!" shouted one of the warriors, shooting down the deadly machine. "There are hundreds of them!"

"Combat robots!" Anamesh murmured, a questioning look on his masked face.

-

Deadly energy beams were firing from the combat robots' formation. More than five hundred of them were advancing against the enemy platoon, outnumbering them twenty to one. Beam after beam cut through the enemy-powered vacuum suits as if they weren't using them.

The Thuban warriors took cover behind pieces of stone and debris left by the nukes.

A few barrages of grenades exploded within the robots' formation, ripping them apart. The Thubans fired their energy weapons non-stop until they realized the enemy surrounded them.

A combat robot engaged in close combat with one Thuban warrior. In rapid movements, both were hitting each other violently. Using his standard retractable sword, the warrior was finding it hard to damage the mechanical being.

The robot hit the lizard in the chest, throwing him over five meters in the air and leaving the warrior motionless on the red ground.

Rapidly, more combat was occurring with identical results.

-

"Retreat!" Anamesh ordered. He was frightened, as the robots were deadly. For the first time in his long life, he had found an enemy even more lethal than he was.

More than twenty warriors opened the path of retreat with their grenades and energy weapons. It had been a mistake to land troops without substantial support. Anamesh expected human resistance, not indestructible automates.

Vegans had hidden assets, once again.

"Keep running!" shouted one of the warriors. He gazed back to see another warrior fall on the ground, a massive cauterized hole in his chest.

-

In space, Third Commander Dracko intently watched the images of the ground battles. Everywhere on the planet, the result was the same. Combat robots were annihilating his troops. "Fire the energy beams against the robots!" he ordered with an infuriated gaze.

"Third Commander, we might kill our troops if we fire upon their positions," Krigi stated, working fervently on his console.

"Do it now!" Dracko replied, aiming a stunner gun directly at Krigi's head.

Krigi remained still for half a second, knowing that if he didn't fire the energy beams, he might be stunned and then spaced through an airlock. "Beams firing."

-

On the ground, bright white flashes began appearing in the sky. Anamesh, who was pushing Ebadan inside a shuttle, knew they would die if they remained on the surface of Mars for a few more seconds. Once everyone was inside the shuttle, the energy screen of the vessel activated, leaving the bright impacts of the robots' blue energy beams glowing intensely against the shield.

The shuttle accelerated rapidly when a powerful energy beam shot from the *Behemoth Ascending* and impacted the area, cleansing over five hundred square meters around it. Instantly, more beams fell from the sky with identical results, destroying most of the enemy robots.

-

"Shuttles are back, sir. Reports said over seventy percent casualties," Tactical Officer Krigi said.

"Sterilize the planet," Dracko ordered angrily, his fangs crunching against each other until purple blood was visible.

Immediately, more than one hundred cluster nuclear warheads left from the *Behemoth Ascending* and the *Ascendant Ripper*. The missiles traveled across the planet's orbit, then began falling onto Mars. Each bomb contained twenty-five tactical nuclear warheads in the fifty-kiloton range. Two thousand five hundred nuclear detonations engulfed the planet, liberating a massive number of radioactive isotopes such as *Xenon* and *Krypton* into the atmosphere. Mushroom-shaped clouds were visible from orbit around the entire red world.

CHAPTER TEN

Commander Padis, Governor of Mars, was in his quarters alone. He was deeply submerged in his thoughts, suicidal ones.

"How did we arrive at this?" he wondered, his face covered by torrents of tears that fell down his cheeks. "It seems everything was coordinated: the pirate attack in Syrius and this brutal invasion. I think the Thubans paid a huge amount of money to the pirates as a diversion. It worked for them."

He was holding an old-model pistol from the period of the great catastrophe in his homeworld. He lifted the gun, switched the weapon from safety to fire and stuck it inside his mouth.

Suddenly, a familiar voice screamed in horror; it was Vera. "No!" she said. "Don't do it!"

Padis felt ashamed, as he hadn't expected Vera to be monitoring his quarters. He took the pistol from his mouth and crumbled. "We've lost everything! There is no future!"

"You are still alive, and I am still here. Therefore, there is a future," Vera said with tears falling down her virtual cheeks. "You are the great Commander Padis! If you are alive, our people will have a future. You saved many lives today as you saved them in the past!"

"A million people died today, a lot of good pilots and personnel. How can I live with that pain?" Padis knelt in front of Vera.

"Convert that pain into something useful. Divert that energy into one thing: vengeance!"

-

A nearby comet was passing by in close approach to Terra. It was a regular visitor every few hundred years. The comet was over ten kilometers wide, a planet killer.

Down in Atlantis, Consul Atlas, Commodore Valentis and Sensor Operator Allumin were the only three survivors. They remained at the Government Palace, as they thought it was the right thing to do. If they were meant to die, they would do so like men and not like cowards. The other personnel had been evacuated hours ago in shuttles. Combat robots were holding positions against Thuban warriors just outside the Palace. Some reports from underground shelters informed of enemy soldiers killing thousands of innocent civilians who had found refuge beneath the city.

"Mars has fallen, Consul," Valentis reported, his voice showing defeat. "The planet has been nuked and sterilized."

Atlas remained silent for a moment. He had one more surprise for the lizards. "Activate the *Doom Plan*, and Commodore, you have to go, as do you, Allumin. A shuttle is waiting in the garden."

"There's no way I'm leaving now, Consul," Valentis said, infuriated. "I am the Fleet Commodore; my duty is to die here!"

"Leave now!" Atlas shouted. "You will be useful to our people in the future. You must survive!"

Valentis remain quiet, thinking about that proposition. If he were to live, he would make sure that he sought revenge in the future, if his plans were put in place. "We'll leave, sir. It was an honor to serve with you."

Acting immediately, both men, Commodore Valentis and Allumin, left the situation room.

-

In the Raman city of Andhakas, Amma was screaming in pain when the reptilian alien tore the skin of her right leg. To keep her awake and to intensify her suffering, he gave her adrenaline, which he was supposed to consume in battle, as that hormone made reptilians feel no fear.

"Kill me, you son of a bitch!" Amma said in agony, her body trembling as the adrenaline invaded her nervous system. She could die of a heart attack or drained off. She just wished to die – the sooner, the better. The alien nailed her to the temple's wall, making her body resemble a cross.

"This is just the beginning," he said in joy and excitement.

-

The close-quarter battle against the robots had been devastating. Ebagesh had suffered over fifty percent casualties in his ranks. The enemy forces numbered just a hundred, and they had managed to annihilate more than a thousand of his warriors. If there were only a thousand robots, he wouldn't have survived the first assault. Luckily, he had amended that mistake by ordering orbital bombardment and reinforcements had arrived shortly after that. The city was in ruins; only a vast palace in the center of the ringed island remained intact. In that building, one life-detection still showed up in the scanners.

"Begin the assault," Ebagesh ordered. He wanted to capture that human.

"Sir, I have a report of underground shelters found with thousands of civilians. The third battalion had massacred them. No survivors left," Second Officer Trexin said excitedly.

"Very well, we'll become rich today!" Ebagesh replied with a grin. "Attack!"

-

The Thuban warriors, wearing their armored battle suits, shot their rocket launchers against the wall that surrounded the Government Palace. Huge explosions carved holes in the wall. Smoke and debris were falling when, from the interior, blue beams began bursting the reptilian warriors.

A small hover tank was shooting its deadly payload of energy beams against the fortified palace. Previously, a tank had proved that it could tear apart an Atlantean killer robot.

Suddenly, a robot appeared holding something over its left shoulder. A chirpy whistle broke into the air, and small missiles were incoming to the hover tank position. The rockets flew in circles, making them hard to target. In a moment, a colossal detonation destroyed the reptilian tank, sending everyone around it into the air. A twenty-meter-wide crater appeared when the smoke vanished.

-

Ebagesh was on the ground, his armored battle suit sparking, as it was damaged. He tried to stand, but a pain in his abdomen prevented that. Slowly, he moved his head down to see the problem and, with his right hand, he touched the area. When he lifted his hand, he saw that a purple liquid covered his claws; it was blood.

"Damn it," he groaned. His breath quickened and his body shook, aghast. "I can't die now."

Around him, there was only death. More warriors were systematically annihilated when a strange noise began sounding in the city. It was an alarm. The sound penetrated his ears, making them sting. Then a voice started speaking in the Atlantean language. "Self-destruction activated. Ten minutes to self-destruction." The message repeated itself every few seconds.

Ebagesh tried once again to stand but a metallic foot held him on the ground. His eyes filled with fear. He struggled in vain to free himself from the enemy combat robot that stared at him with the red lights that served as his eyes. The robot shook his head a bit and aimed at Ebagesh's head.

"No!" Ebagesh said, but it was too late.

The robot shot his energy rifle and killed the reptilian officer.

-

Inside the situation room, Consul Atlas had just one more thing to do: press the red button on his table. He was about to die and, once again, Atlanteans were on the brink of extinction.

"How big is that comet?" Atlas asked the computer program in charge of the system, fearing he was about to commit a terrible error, one that could bring a massive extinction event to the planet. However, his desire for revenge had blinded him after he had lost his daughter in the battle over Terra.

"Just over ten kilometers, Consul. It's a planet killer," said the computer in its monotone voice. It wasn't an AI, but it was still an excellent intelligence program.

"Will we be able to bring down the whole comet?" Atlas said.

"No," answered the computer. "Perhaps a big piece of it. Our ground missiles will partially tear it apart, but we don't have the firepower to change its trajectory."

"That would be enough to make the planet uninhabitable for the lizards for at least a thousand years. The temperature will plunge abruptly, and the geography of the planet will change. Let's hope some people survived in Mars and the people we saved in the shuttles will come back better prepared by then," Consul Atlas said, looking at the countdown in its last seconds. "It was a pleasure to serve this world. See you on the other side, my beloved daughter."

Consul Atlas pressed the red button on his table.

-

On board the *Thuban Executor*, High Commander Enki watched in shock through the cockpit window of his Command Center as an enormous mushroom-shaped cloud rose over the city of Atlantis, while another one rose over Poseidonia. He couldn't believe that these Vegans had acted in that manner.

"According to our visual reports, the Vegans activated a self-destruction nuclear device in the twenty-megaton range, annihilating both cities and all around it. Sixty percent of our troops have perished," Second Commander Marduk said, working at his console fervently.

"Damn Vegans!" Enki shouted in wrath, hitting an officer who was sitting next to his position.

"High Commander!" Sensor Officer Okyd said, alarmed. "I am picking up missile launches from the surface, four hundred signals detected and rising."

"What?" Enki moaned in disbelief, his eyes open wide. "What are they targeting?"

"Most of them are heading to that comet," Ynnie said.

"And the rest?" Marduk said, thinking they were the target.

At that moment, almost a hundred nuclear missiles began a parabolic maneuver and began descending to the planet in different locations.

"They're targeting the planet in every location we sent ground troops," Okyd reported, the frown on his face deepening.

-

Amma was semi-unconscious, as she had lost much blood. The reptilian was skinning her slowly and drinking her blood to get high. The alien was a vicious creature, and it was at that moment that Amma understood why the locals called them *evil ones*.

Unexpectedly, the alien stopped his malicious torture and began speaking through his comm device. Amma could hear a low voice in the Thuban language, which she understood correctly. Then she laughed out loud.

"Did you think you could have this planet again? Now you're going to taste some of your own medicine, you son of a bitch," she said, laughing at the frightened alien, who left the place running.

A second later, over the city of Andhakas, an Atlantean missile appeared, triggering a nuclear detonation that swept across the area, razing every inhabitant and alien invader in it.

-

It was too late for the Thuban fleet to intercept the missiles targeting the comet. They were too far out to reach it. Once the rockets left the planet's atmosphere, the mini sub-light drives they had installed went online. In a matter of minutes, they found their target.

The comet exploded in bright light, tearing apart into many big pieces and leaving another one over six kilometers wide continuing on its trajectory. A few of those smaller pieces entered the atmosphere, the biggest one being over one kilometer wide. The planet was still under nuclear fire and multiple mushroom-shaped clouds could be seen from the *Thuban Executor*.

"They won," said Second Officer Ynnie, almost whispering.

Everyone watched in shock and anger as pieces of the comet entered the atmosphere. One of them was much more visible than the others.

"Report impact course of that big chunk!" Second Commander Marduk ordered, breathing rapidly.

"Northern ice cap, Commander," reported Sensor Officer Okyd.

More than twenty impacts of different sizes and magnitudes hit the ice cap that covered most of the northern hemisphere. The reaction was horrendous. Bright lights emerged from the planet. Pieces of ice the size of a small mountain arrived in the stratosphere and then fell to the surface. Trillions of gallons of water instantly evaporated and a tremendous amount that melted, enough to fill the Mediterranean Sea, poured into the ocean and continents' coastal shores. The tectonic plates couldn't resist the energy released after the comet's impacts on the four-kilometer-thick icecaps and rotated a few degrees south, triggering a catastrophic chain of events. All over the planet, volcanoes erupted, while mega-tsunamis rose in every ocean, razing everything. Soon, ash and pollutants from the nuclear bombs and volcanic activity would submerge Terra in a nuclear winter that could last for hundreds of years.

The Atlanteans, instead of surrendering and serving the planet on a platter for the invaders, preferred to destroy it and leave it uninhabitable for as long as possible.

High Commander Enki couldn't believe what had just happened.

Shortly after that, a few remaining Atlantean shuttles left the planet from the southern continent of Antarctica. Once free of the atmosphere, they entered hyperspace.

A one-thousand-meter tsunami swept over the city of Atlantis – what was left of it. In just twenty-four hours, the worldwide sea level rose over a hundred and twenty meters.

The Atlanteans had been defeated this time, but they would return one day.

EPILOGUE

High Commander Enki was on his way back to Thuban Prime. The Atlanteans had submerged the gold planet in a nuclear winter, and the climate was so adverse for his race that he had decided to leave that world, at least for now.

"The Council will be furious about our defeat," Second Commander Marduk said, fearing that this trip would be the last he would ever take.

"We haven't been defeated!" Enki grumbled, looking for a long moment at the bright, colorful lights of hyperspace. "We are going to return. Then we will conquer this cursed planet forever."

Marduk remained silent for a moment. "What if no humans have survived on the surface? Who is going to extract the gold?"

"We will bring slaves from one of our slave-worlds to do that job," Enki replied. "For now, let's get home and deal with the Council. It is our time to rise in power."

Enki had great plans for his clan, and for himself. Nothing would stop him from accomplishing them.

-

Vera, the AI in charge of the Titan Project, was shocked when she saw, on some viewscreens beside Commander Padis, the destruction that had occurred on Mars and the apocalyptic end of Terra. Atlantis, Poseidonia, Agartha, Triton, Cepheus and Ceres were destroyed. All mining operations on the planet were annihilated, ending her mission of turning Mars into a garden once again, at least for now. She wasn't human, but she was designed to feel like one and to develop her feelings withing a limit; she couldn't harm any Atlanteans, only traitors to her race.

"What now? What will happen to us?" Vera asked softly, barely understanding the situation.

"We have saved more than ten thousand people in this complex. We will put them asleep, including me, and wait until everything is over," Commander Padis said in resignation.

"What about me?" Vera asked sadly. "I don't want to be alone."

"You can go sleep too," Commander Padis told her, looking straight into her dark eyes. "I wish I could hug you now."

For the first time, Vera felt the human emotion of hopelessness. Tears fell down the cheeks of her holographic image. "I wish that too, Commander. Perhaps in the future," she said with a small, sad grin.

"Program the computers to monitor all that will be possible during the time we will be gone. If anything changes, you will wake up first, evaluate the situation and then take me out of the dreamless darkness I am entering. Do you understand, Vera?" Padis asked, this time in a firm voice. If they were awakened at the wrong moment, there was a chance that they wouldn't be able to go back to sleep for a long time, and food and water were limited.

"Understood, Commander. Good sleep and see you soon," Vera replied. Her image disappeared.

"See you soon, my child," Padis said. For him, the AI was his never-born daughter.

With a deep sadness, Vera monitored everyone while they entered the cryo capsules. In that moment, she decided that if they woke up again, she would transfer her program – or soul, as she liked to call it – int a synthetic body. She would hug Commander Padis and perhaps give him the love he had never received from a son or daughter.

An hour later, everyone in the Titan Complex was asleep, and the lights and systems were shut down. Vera closed her eyes and her soul went idle.

THE END

If you have enjoyed *Solaris Fall: Behemoth Ascending Novellas Part One*, please post a review and leave some stars. Good reviews encourage an author to write and improve, and they help sell books. Reviews can be just a few short sentences, describing what you liked about the book.

Please note that this is my first published novella and English isn't my mother tongue. If you have suggestions, please contact me at my website, whose link appears below or leave a review with your concerns. Thank you for reading *Solaris Fall: Behemoth Ascending Series Novellas Part One* and being so supportive. For updates on current writing projects and future publications, visit my author website. Also, sign up for notifications when my new books come out on Amazon.

Website: frankjmanchon.wordpress.com

Follow me on Facebook at Frank J. Manchon.

Turn the page for an introduction to the first book of *Behemoth Ascending,* which will be released sometime on Summer 2019.

BEHEMOTH

ASCENDING

BOOK ONE

"Violence is the last refuge

of the incompetent."

ISAAC ASIMOV

PROLOGUE

Eight years of service in the United States Space Marine Force. Eight years of hard training and space travel between Earth and Luna had prepared him for this day. So many years had been wasted for nothing. No one could prepare a Marine for what was coming after him. Fighting another human was one thing but fighting an unknown enemy with far superior weapons and combat skills was another. This enemy was made for one thing and one thing only: war.

Captain Mark Mason, from the USSMF, couldn't believe what was coming up behind him. Half of his squad was dead; Lieutenant Brooks, Sergeant Newton and Private Mendez had been slaughtered in a matter of seconds. They hadn't had a chance to defend themselves. Only Private Perez was alive and waiting in the security of the Mars Rover outside the dark cavern. He knew that Commander Officer Alexander Rodker would be furious about this outcome. The Commander was, at that moment, exploring the Cydonia Mensae site, just over two hundred kilometers from the crash site, doing some research with other members of the MarX Mission, determining whether Cydonia had once been inhabited and whether those stone formations were, indeed, remains of a civilization.

He kept running just behind Sergeant Miller while he set up automatic high explosive charges along the last corridor before exiting the dark and dangerous place. What he saw inside that place would rewrite the history books. There was life in all kinds of forms.

The mission should have been a standard reconnaissance mission. Just get to the target, evaluate the level of danger, explore and secure the area — no chance of that. Getting inside the spacecraft wasn't easy. The only visible entrance was a dark cavern just beneath the cliff side of a valley. Captain Mason thought the cavern entrance wasn't natural, as the circular shape indicated it had been drilled. After a few minutes inside the spacecraft, trouble began with a fatal result.

"Keep moving, Sergeant!" Mason ordered through the radio comm device installed in his pressurized combat helmet. "Last two charges, first one to detonate in five seconds, following ones after two seconds."

"Yes, sir," Sergeant Miller replied, breathing intensely. Gravity on Mars was a third of Earth's normal gravity. That was why the Marines had been equipped with heavier gear and weapons. All equipment was heavy, but Marines were tough guys.

The creature that followed them was over fifty meters behind. After killing the other members of the squad, the terrifying monster remained for a precious couple of minutes, dismembering the three unlucky men piece by piece. It was vicious, even worse than the darkest serial killer or the wildest and most ferocious predator in the savanna. Mason saw it all, and it almost made him vomit –not a good idea in a vacuum battle suit. He was petrified and wrath boiled his blood. He shot the creature with many bursts of piercing rounds, but the bullets had no effect. A heavily armored battle suit protected the alien. Mason knew that close combat was out of the question. The damn thing was over seven feet tall, with a firm complexion and the most shocking thing – a long and lethal tail. Mason wondered whether the alien was reptilian, as the shape of its helmet gave him that impression. In that moment, he felt powerless. It was as though all the training he'd had over the years to fight this thing was useless. He felt like a small antelope trying to fight a hungry lion.

Finally, the first high explosive detonation blew up. Captain Mason and Sergeant Miller heard a scream while the ground shook lightly. Both were close to the entrance of the cavern; just a hundred more meters to run in darkness. Then the second explosion detonated, shaking the ground, this time more than the previous detonation. Dust and small pieces of debris fell all over the place. Then came the third explosion and the fourth. The whole area began to crumble, and big chunks of rock fell from the top. Smaller pieces hit both marines, making Mason fall on his knees, though he immediately stood back up.

"I think we got the motherfucking bastard! It must pay for what it did to our bros!" Miller shouted in jubilation, a touch of revenge in his voice.

"I hope you're right," Mason was replying when, from behind, a small energy burst brushed his head, almost impacting him. In a quick movement, he turned his eyes to Sergeant Miller as his comm fell silent with just static. He saw the body fall to the floor, beheaded, with no sign of blood gushing out of his neck. The energy burst had cauterized the wound. His heart practically stopped. His run ended when he turned around and pulled his heavy assault rifle to his shoulder. Furiously, he faced the alien and pulled the trigger. He screamed nonstop as more piercing rounds left the rifle's cannon. Empty cases impacted the ground and the walls of the cavern, creating remarkable metal clinks. Tears ran down Sergeant Mason's cheeks, as he had known Sergeant Miller for several years. They had been good friends, and Mason knew that Miller had two kids, with one having just been born. How could he tell Miller's wife Emily that a vicious alien had beheaded her husband? That was, assuming he survived this mission.

Piercing round after piercing round left the rifle's cannon in a burst of fire. The chemical composition inside the cartridge cases was slightly different from that used on Earth, as Mars had almost no oxygen with which to burn gunpowder. The alien screamed. Violent moves and screams indicated that a few projectiles had succeeded in penetrating the alien's battle armor. The noise was deafening, reminding Mason of a dinosaur from a movie. The high explosive detonations had partially damaged the powerful armor that the alien wore. Energy bursts kept coming out of the alien's weapon but did not hit the human. Mason finally emptied his rifle's magazine of its five hundred bullets. Then, with a deep breath and a wolfish look, he grabbed a detonator with his left hand. The last high explosive wasn't activated by movement; this one was a remote-control detonation device, and the goddamn alien was right next to it. The alien was fighting to remain on his feet. Looking at the human, he dropped his weapon in a sign of surrender when Mason pressed the button. "See you in hell, son of a bitch."

CHAPTER ONE

One month earlier

Inside the MarX Transit 1, Commander Officer Alexander Rodker was looking out the cockpit window in the command center to see, for the first time through a human eye, the red planet. The view was astonishing, breath-taking. The dream of Mars was closer than ever. Too many questions without answers awaited them on that planet. It was the only chance for humanity to survive in the long term; humanity needed a second home to avoid a future extinction. Pollution, war and overpopulation were decimating the world's natural resources and ecosystems. Mass extinctions of species were occurring, with several species disappearing daily from the face of the Earth. The rain forest was cut down to allow for more intensive farming to feed a hungry and unstoppably rising population that had just exceeded the ten billion mark. In another twenty years, the population would rise to twelve billion and, by the end of the century, to twenty billion. Space travel and colonization of the solar system was a priority to avoid the destruction – the self-destruction – of the human race.

The small fleet heading to the red planet needed another few days before it began the deceleration phase and then executed hyperbolic entry into Mars' thin atmosphere. It had taken six months for the crew of the first human mission to arrive at their destination. In those months, the one hundred and forty members of the four manned spacecraft had prepared for what would come next: building a human settlement, expanding the propellant plant already working on the planet and sending the spacecraft back to Earth. The other spacecraft, BMR Class (Big Methane Rocket), were the MarX Transit 2 and two cargo ships with all the supplies they would need when more colonists and equipment arrived throughout the two-year mission. To minimize the travel time to the planet, Mission Control, based in Houston, had to wait until Mars was near its closest orbit to Earth. The next window, when they could return the cargo and the transit crafts, would take two years to arrive. In that time, many things could go wrong, perhaps so badly that some would lose their lives. There was a risk, yes, but every crew member had agreed to accept it.

-

Days later, the comm console in the quarters went on. "Sir, we're approaching the orbit of Mars. Hyperbolic entry is set up for ten hours," reported the Comm Officer.

"Copy that, I'll be there in thirty minutes," replied Commander Alexander Rodker, pressing the comm button of his quarter.

He tried to stand so that he could put on a clean uniform, but the microgravity was giving him a hard time. He couldn't wait until he felt gravity again. Even though Mars had only a third of Earth's gravity, the prospect of standing erect on the planet's dusty ground made him feel better. A larger spacecraft with a self-rotating wheel that created artificial gravity was under construction on Luna Space Station, but it would take several more years to finish the titanic craft. Rodker looked at himself in a mirror on the wall. "I need to shave this beard. I can't go live on every media site around the world and look like a homeless person," he thought while touching his one-month growth of beard.

Thirty minutes later, he arrived at the Command Center to check all the systems before initiating the final approach to the planet and begin the landing. If every-thing went right, the landing stage would take over five minutes. The landing site selected for this mission was in Cydonia Mensae, a bit far from the planet's equator, where temperatures were far better than the sub-zero temperatures they would find in Cydonia. That con-cerned him, as it was a change of plans from those of just one month earlier. Once on the surface, they'd settle in-side a shallow crater, where the crew would install a provisional habitation dome while the underground ones were constructed to protect them from the lethal solar radiation. The cavity was just a few miles from where the Viking probe had taken a photo of a mysteri-ous human face and what looked like a pyramid com-plex. That complex wasn't like the Giza pyramids, which resembled the Orion belt; this one resembled the Pleiades constellation. Perhaps it was a clear message for humanity, a clue as to its origin or, something worse, a warning. That concerned Rodker immensely. He was sure that Mars had once had a civilization, possibly hu-man-like, and that all those details had been kept secret from the public. Of course, conspiratorial theorists all around the world didn't buy it. For them, it was utterly impossible that geology had created those structures naturally.

"What's the status?" asked Rodker of XO Captain Cartwright as he sat on his command chair.

"All systems are fully working, sir," answered the handsome young Captain.

"The other ships?" Rodker asked, touching several icons on the control screen.

"All functional, nothing to worry about," Cartwright replied.

Ensign Tanaka turned to Rodker. "It's been a hell of a ride, hasn't it?"

"Yes, it has," replied Rodker, rolling his eyes. "We all spent some time in the ISS, but this..." he paused. "This has been a damn nightmare. I hope to remain on Mars, not have another trip like this one."

Everyone nodded, agreeing with the Commander. Almost fifty people in a small vessel like that one, sharing four crew members a quarter. It was worse than the military training period when dozens of recruits had to share a small barracks.

"Sir," said Lieutenant Ravenna, "do you believe there was a civilization on Mars?"

Rodker looked down and then at the Lieutenant. "Perhaps. If there once was one, we'll find out soon."

-

Hours later, the four crewed vessels, the MarX Transit Vehicle 1 and 2 and the two cargo ships, identical to the Transit ones but carrying only a heavy payload, made their final approach toward the Martian orbit. The deceleration phase finished and, using just thrusters, the ships took their position to enter the thin CO_2 atmosphere of the planet.

"This is Commander Officer Alexander Rodker from the MarX Transit 1. We're about to initiate the landing sequence. We're here, in Mars, and if everything goes as planned, we should be on the planet's surface in the next five to six minutes," said Rodker into the camera that was recording the whole process and broadcasting it on every media site in the world. "On my mark." He took a deep breath. "Begin the landing sequence."

Everyone in the busy and small Command Center of the MarX Transit 1 began pressing icons on their station's computer screens.

"EDL (Entry, descend, landing) sequence engaged, all systems functioning correctly," said Captain Cartwright.

"Helmets on and security belts fastened tightly," ordered Rodker. He could feel the ship shaking slightly.

"Altitude, four hundred, and fifty kilometers and descending," said Sensor Officer Ensign Tanaka. Seconds later, the spacecraft began shaking much more strongly than before due to the ship's contact with the atmosphere. "Two hundred kilometers and descending."

"Vectors are looking good," said Captain Cartwright. "Constant velocity descends balanced. The temperature in the hull, seventeen thousand Celsius."

Rodker continued looking at the central command view screen for all the details. One small error in the descending sequence and the ships could turn into fireballs.

"Ten seconds for thrusters, propellant valves functioning," said Lieutenant Ravenna, prepared to press the thruster's icon. "Thrusters firing."

Moments after firing the thrusters, the spacecraft turned ninety degrees, fired the propulsive engines and opened the air brakes. The high G level made the crew feel significant pressure on their chests, like someone was standing on them.

"Twenty kilometers and descending, thirty seconds for a touchdown," Ensign Tanaka said. Everyone was anxious to touch the ground. It had been a long trip, and a successful landing would be their prize. "Touchdown in three, two, one..." Slowly, the spacecraft opened its landing legs and touched the dusty ground. A sudden and violent movement hit the vessel and then nothing. "Landing successful, turning off engines."

A second of silence reigned. Then, explosions of jubilation filled the Command Center.

"Status of the other ships?" Rodker asked, his heartbeat increasing.

"MarX Transit 2 touched down, Cargo 1 touched down, Cargo 2..." Captain Cartwright suddenly stopped, her face turning pale. "I have no contact with Cargo 2. It doesn't appear in the sensors, and I have no link to it."

Rodker felt his heart stop for a moment. A chill ran through his body. "Contact Transit 2 and scan the surface, now!"

"Sir, Transit 2 at the comm," reported Captain Cartwright.

Rodker lifted his arm and pressed the comm button. "Here, Commander Rodker, what's your status."

"Here, Second Commander Aiden Godley. Cargo 2 disintegrated when it touched the atmosphere. We saw it with our own eyes, sir," the Second Commander reported in a sad, deep voice.

"Are you sure about that?" Rodker asked. He couldn't believe he had lost a cargo ship. Even though he had a second ship with the exact same payload, the loss meant they would have to be extremely careful with the remaining resources.

"Completely sure, Sir," Godley replied.

"Understood, commander." Rodker took a few seconds to think about the consequences of that catastrophe. The idea of sending two cargo ships with the mission was simple. If one cargo ship was destroyed, the second one, carrying the same payload as the first, would sustain the mission. On the other hand, four cargo ships had arrived previously with some necessities the crew would need for the two-year mission, but the main payload of that previous uncrewed mission was the automated propellant plant and the solar power plant to operate it. "Prepare your crew to disembark."

-

Back on Earth, the news of the destroyed cargo ship felt like a splash of cold water. Isaac Wyse, President, and CEO of OmegaTech, the technological giant, was in the main hall of his company's headquarters in Houston, Texas, in front of more than two thousand guests, including heads of state, NASA representatives, scientists and hundreds of reporters for news channels. Everyone was paralyzed at the words of Second Commander Godley. There was a delay of several minutes in the video feed due to the distance between Earth and Mars. Wyse then coughed lightly and took the microphone.

"Well, ladies and gentlemen, we're on Mars." The attendees of the event, the most important one in human history, were a bit confused. Some were applauding, others looking at each other in dismay. "The mission has been a success. As explained on many occasions, accidents may occur, as what we're trying to accomplish has never been done. The surviving cargo is all that's necessary to proceed and complete the mission. Both cargoes were identical; we provided them both simply as a precaution. Do not panic; the crew is safe on the Martian surface. We should be receiving video feed of the crew stepping outside. Neil Armstrong made a little step for man and a huge step for humanity; well, we have made history today. This is not a small step, this is a huge jump."

The attendees realized that he was right; the mission was a success and they must celebrate. Jubilation erupted when, suddenly, Mr. Wyse granted a question from a young and beautiful journalist.

"Good afternoon, Mr. Wyse. I am Rebecca Hernandez from Channel 4. My question is a bit controversial. Was it decided to change the landing site of the mission from the equatorial area to the freezing Cydonia Mensae because you and the government want to find out whether the Pyramid Complex in there proves the existence of alien life?" The journalist was known in the news world as one of the most controversial journalists. That reputation gave her millions of social media followers around the world.

Isaac Wyse grinned. "Well, Miss Hernandez, once again you are misinformed. There isn't a pyramid complex in Mars, just a natural formation of rocks in that area."

Hernandez interrupted. "That isn't what the satellite images show us. A natural formation of rocks, as you called it, doesn't resemble the Pleiades Constellation. Do you deny this information in front of the world, as well as the Oumuamua incident?"

Wyse looked confused, but then answered. "I do not deny anything, as I can't confirm it. I promise you, if that formation turns out to be a pyramid, I will inform the world about it. Moreover, for your information, I don't know what you're talking about in terms of the Oumuamua incident, if I pronounced it correctly."

Suddenly, Commander Rodker's video feed appeared on the gigantic view screen in the hall, just behind Isaac Wyse. He interrupted the daring journalist. "Well, I have no idea what to say at this moment. I had tried to prepare these words for over six months, and now my mind is blank. So, to all inhabitants of Earth, this is for you." Rodker began descending the few steps separating the spacecraft from the Martian ground. The view was astonishing; several red hills were visible, with a partially red sky and little CO_2 clouds on the horizon. Rodker stood still on the last step. Everyone in the event room was silent. Their hearts were racing as fast as steam trains. "Humanity has arrived in a new world. We're an interplanetary species now," Rodker said when he finally stepped onto the surface of Mars.

History would forever remember him as a brave pioneer who had conquered a new world. More cheers of jubilation erupted in the room. Bottles of champagne opened everywhere, and many of the attendees hugged each other. It was a gigantic event, the most important one since the Moon Landing back in the twentieth century.

"Ladies and gentlemen, mission accomplished," said Isaac Wyse. Moments later, in a closed microphone, he said to one of his assistants, "Find the source of the attack in the cargo ship." The assistant nodded and left the site.

-

In a conference room under the Cheyenne Mountains, Isaac Wyse was discussing the situation in Mars with the government's cabinet and President Sarah Powell.

"All we know is," said Wyse, "that a kind of energy weapon destroyed my cargo ship when it entered the Martian atmosphere." He paused. "I wonder what the hell is going on. I lost millions of dollars in that ship."

Secretary of Defense General Joshua Sonnet looked up at Wyse and opened a folder, one of the secret ones, then addressed him. "Mr. Wyse, you don't have the security clearance for this classified information. That is the reason why you did not know anything. However, in this situation, we need to inform you." Sonnet stopped to pass Wyse a confidentiality contract. Wyse read it carefully. "Once you sign it, I will inform you of everything we know, as we have no choice. We need your help."

After a few minutes, Wyse signed the contract. He didn't hesitate in doing so, as he was getting impatient to know why he had lost a spacecraft. Luckily, no humans had been in it. "I'm all ears."

General Sonnet then addressed him about the situation regarding the Oumuamua incident and much more, such as Roswell and some evidence of a human-like civilization, extrasolar in origin, that had once inhabited Earth and Mars, as well as possibly other planets and moons across the solar system. "What is on Mars, it had been here before. All our data said that they left the planet about four thousand years ago, when someone from outer space drove them out of our planet," General Sonnet said.

Wyse remained silent. He was a bit pale, as he was shocked by the disclosure of the information he had just received. Then he was infuriated. He had lost a space-craft, and the government would pay for it. It was without a doubt the biggest cover-up in human history. "Explain something to me. Why on Earth have I not been informed of this? I sent people there, for God's sake!" he said with increasing ferocity in his voice.

"Because if something goes wrong, it will be your fault, not ours," replied President Powell calmly. "That's why we invested a lot of taxpayer money in your companies. We cannot afford the blame for such a cover-up."

Wyse, smashing his fists against the table, said, "This is fucking unbelievable. You used me as a scapegoat for your dirty business. What if that supposed enemy returns to Earth? Do you have the ability to stop them? Or are you going to blame me for the fact that they may come back?"

"We can't stop such a threat. That's why we are asking you for help," Vice President Sherry Campbell calmly intervened.

"This is unbelievable. I'm your scapegoat and also your only hope of cleaning up your mess." Wyse lifted his hand to his forehead. With a despairing look at the ceiling, he laughed. "You must be kidding me!"

"Mr. Wyse, calm down," said General Sonnet. "We have an inside military team among your crew. We need to explore the ruins in Cydonia Mensae and the spaceship as well. We need your cooperation."

If you liked this, it will be available on Amazon soon!

13615668R00089

Printed in Germany
by Amazon Distribution
GmbH, Leipzig